向A咖西洋歌手學英文

巨星的
人生故事與名言

EZ TALK 編輯部

Judd Piggott、James Baron

著

使用
說明

From Kosovo to Global Pop Sensation

They say the apple doesn't fall far from the tree, and that [1)] **definitely** of Dua Lipa. Her father had enjoyed success as the [LG]**lead** band Oda in his native [LG]**Kosovo**. In addition to *honing his [2)]**craft** at home, he played CDs featuring songs by [3)]**legendary** artists like Bob Dylan, David Bowie and Radiohead. Growing up in this environment, it seemed natural that Dua Lipa would **follow suit**.

有其父必有其女，這句話用來形容杜娃黎波再貼切不過了。她父親曾是搖滾樂團 唱，在家鄉科索沃小有名氣。平常在家除了精進歌藝也會播放 CD 唱片，聽一 巴布狄倫、大衛鮑伊和電台司令的歌。耳濡目染之下，杜娃黎波跟隨父親的腳 然的事。

By the age of six, Dua Lipa was already showing a gift for perform along to her favorite songs. She [4)]**cites** singer [LG]**Pink** as a major influence. Yet Lipa's dreams suffered an early *blow e was a primary school student in London. While auditioning for the s [5)]**choir**, she was told by music teachers that her voice was too low to hit the high notes. In fact, the teachers went further, saying the young student lacked the talent to be a singer.

杜娃黎波六歲時就展現出表演能力，能夠跟著自己最愛的音樂哼唱。她提到自己深受粉紅佳 人影響，然而她的夢想在小時候就遭到打擊，那時她在倫敦念小學。她參加學校合唱團的徵 選，音樂老師說她的聲線太低了，唱不了高音。事實上，老師還說這位年幼學生沒有當歌手 的天賦。

> 7000字以外
> 的單字，以
> ★ 呈現。

> 選字範圍為
> 4000-7000
> 字，以標號
> 方式呈現。

VOCABULARY

1. **definitely** [ˈdɛfənɪtli] (adv.) 一定地，絕對地
2. **craft** [kræft] (n) 才藝
3. **legendary** [ˈlɛdʒənˌdɛri] (a.) 傳說中的，著名的
4. **cite** [saɪt] (v.) 舉例，引用
5. **choir** [kwaɪr] (n.) 合唱團，唱詩班

ADVANCED WORDS

★ **hone** [hon] (v.) 磨練
★ **blow** [blo] (n.) 打擊

Dua Lipa 杜娃黎波　**33**

LANGUAGE GUIDE (LG)

Fifteen years later, those *naysayers **have egg on their faces**. Ignoring their [1)]**criticism**, Dua Lipa has achieved international *superstardom. In fact, her deep voice has become her [2)]**trademark**.

十五年後，那些唱衰她的人如今顏面盡失。杜娃黎波無視他們的批評，成為國際超級巨星。 事實上，她那低沉渾厚的嗓音反倒成了她的註冊商標。

It's not surprising that Lipa was able to overcome these problems, given the [3)]**determination** she showed from a young age. In 2008, her parents returned to their birthplace, Pristina, the capital of Kosovo. The country had just gained independence and after a bloody war. Although her family wasn't affected by the violence personally, she has classmates who suffered. Yet she found Pristina "way safer" than London, and remembers her time there fondly. He [LG]**Albanian** improved, she learned about [LG]**Kosovar** culture, and she made c When hip hop stars like Snoop Dogg and 50 Cent performed in Pristina, Lipa was able to attend their concerts, thanks to her father's connections.

黎波小小年紀就展現決心，克服這些問題並不令人意外。2008 年，她的父母搬回出生地， 科索沃的首都普里斯蒂納居住。科索沃才剛經歷一場血戰取得獨立。雖然她家並沒有受到暴 力事件影響，卻有同學慘遭苦難。儘管如此，她還是覺得普里斯蒂納比倫敦「安全得多」， 深深懷念那裡的時光。她的阿爾巴尼亞語進步了（阿爾巴尼亞語和科索沃的官方語言之 一），也認識了科索沃文化，交了一些好朋友。當史努比狗狗和五角這些嘻哈歌手到普里斯 蒂納演出時，她也藉著父親的關係得以觀賞他們的演唱會。

VOCABULARY

1. **criticism** [ˈkrɪtəˌsɪzəm] (n.) 批評，評論

2. **trademark** [ˈtred.mɑrk] (n.) 招牌，代表性物品

3. **determination** [dɪˌtɝmɪˈneʃən] (n.) 堅毅，決心

4. **career** [kəˈrɪr] (n.) 職業，生涯

5. **enroll** [ɪnˈrol] (v.) (註冊) 入學

6. **website** [ˈwɛb.saɪt] (n.) (電腦) 網站

7. **agency** [ˈedʒənsi] (n.) 經紀公司，代理商

lead vocalist 主唱
又可稱為 main vocalist 或是 lead singer， 是在音樂團體中負責主要歌唱部份的成 員，他們負責的部分旋律較為突出，主唱 可能被視為樂團的靈魂或代言人。

rock 搖滾樂
起源於四〇年代末期英國和美國，五〇年 代開始大為風行，為 rock and roll 的簡稱。 現在的搖滾樂泛指所具備搖滾風格的樂 曲。

Kosovo 科索沃 / Albanian 阿爾巴尼亞語
位在歐洲巴爾幹半島的國家，在 1990 年代 末期透過戰爭脫離塞爾維亞並宣布獨立， 但塞爾維亞至今仍不承認其獨立，故時有 衝突。Kosovar 為科索沃人，或科索沃相 關事物，阿爾巴尼亞語 (Albanian) 為科索 沃的官方語言之一。

SoundCloud
線上音樂串流平臺，總部位於德國柏林， 供音樂人上傳自操，使用者可關注和轉發。 平臺於 2007 年創立，已發展為最大的音樂 串流媒體服務商之一。

disco 迪斯可音樂
是一種舞曲音樂，特點是強勁的節拍和穩 定的節奏，常伴隨合成器和電子鼓，來自 1970 年美國盛行，以其歡快的節奏、朗朗 上口的旋律和重複的歌詞而聞名。

出

場中短暫出現的演員 cameo role。用法是 Sb. meo in... 或是 Sb. makes pearance in... 這個字也

信

發表的一封信。
，但內容公開
，通常是為了抗議

Gaza 加薩走廊
位於埃及和以色列中間，為 Gaza Strip（加 薩走廊）的簡稱。由於長年伊斯蘭歷史因素， 為以色列和巴勒斯坦武力爭取的土地，衝 突不斷。

功力與幸辣教育的形象受到讚譽。賈維 是榮獲「最佳搖滾女歌手」 全英最樂獎 「最佳國際女藝人」等多項大獎。

向 A 咖西洋歌手學英文　**34**

Dua Lipa 杜娃黎波　**39**

> 文章內關鍵術語與歌手音樂靈感來源都
> 會在 LANGUAGE GUIDE 裡補充説明。

🔊 09 | 全文閱讀
🔊 10 | 單字

From Kosovo to Global Pop Sensation

They say the apple doesn't fall far from the tree, and that's ¹⸍ᴰ**definitely** true of Dua Lipa. Her father had enjoyed success as the ᴸᴰ**lead vocalist** of ᴸᴰ**rock band** Oda in his native ᴸᴰ**Kosovo**. In addition to *****honing** his ²**craft** at home, he played CDs featuring songs by ³**legendary** artists like Bob Dylan, David Bowie and Radiohead. Growing up in this environment, it seemed natural that Dua Lipa would **follow suit**.

有其父必有其女，這句話用來形容杜娃黎波再貼切不過了。她父親曾是搖滾樂團 Oda 的主唱，在家鄉科索沃小有名氣。平常在家除了精進歌藝他會播放 CD 唱片，一些傳奇歌手如巴布狄倫、大衛鮑伊和電台司令的歌。耳濡目染之下，杜娃黎波跟隨父親的腳步似乎是很自然的事。

By the age of six, Dua Lipa was already showing a gift for performance, singing along to her favorite songs. She ⁶**cites** singer ᴸᴰ**Pink** as a major influence. Yet Lipa's dreams suffered an early *****blow** while she was a primary school student in London. While auditioning for the school ⁵**choir**, she was told by music teachers that her voice was too low to hit the high notes. In fact, the teachers went further, saying the young student lacked the talent to be a singer.

杜娃黎波六歲時就展現出表演力，能夠跟著自己最愛的音樂哼唱。她提到自己深受粉紅佳人影響。然而她的夢想在小時候就遭到打擊，那時她在倫敦念小學。她參加學校合唱團的徵選，音樂老師說她的聲線太低了，唱不到高音。事實上，老師還說過這位年幼學生沒有當歌手的天賦。

VOCABULARY

1. **definitely** [ˋdɛfənɪtlɪ] (adv.) 一定地，絕對地
2. **craft** [kræft] (n.) 才藝
3. **legendary** [ˋlɛdʒən͵dɛrɪ] (a.) 傳說中的、著名的
4. **cite** [saɪt] (v.) 舉例，引用
5. **choir** [kwaɪr] (n.) 合唱團，唱詩班

ADVANCED WORDS

* **hone** [hon] (v.) 磨練
* **blow** [blo] (n.) 打擊

Dua Lipa 杜娃黎波 **33**

PHRASES

the apple doesn't fall far from the tree 有其父（母）必有其子（女）

此片語字面上的意思為「蘋果落地後，離樹不遠」，引申為孩子和父母的個性與資質相似，也就是「有其父（母）必有其子（女）」。

A I notice this new product is available in lots of supermarkets now.
　我注意到這個新產品現在在很多超市都有販售。

B Yup. After the first store started selling it, the others quickly **followed suit**.
　對啊，第一家店開始賣後，其他店很快就開始仿效。

某人做了愚蠢的事，就可以用 have egg on one's face 來形容。

A My friend said I would fail this exam!
　我朋友說我這次考試會不及格！

B I guess he **had egg on his face** when you got such a high grade.
　我猜他在你得了這麼高分後一定感到很尷尬。

follow suit 仿效，跟風

suit 的意思為「同花色的一組紙牌」，follow suit 就是跟著別人的花色出牌，也可引伸為「跟風」，和別人一起，一窩蜂做一樣的事，就可用 follow suit。

A I notice this new product is available in lots of supermarkets now.
　我注意到這個新產品現在在很多超市都有販售。

B Yup. After the first store started selling it, the others quickly **followed suit**.
　對啊，第一家店開始賣後，其他店很快就開始仿效。

40 向 A 咖西洋歌手學英文

A Felix is really good at tennis, just like his father.
　費利克斯在網球方面真的很厲害，就像他父親一樣。

B Well, **the apple doesn't fall far from the tree**.
　嗯，果然有其父必有其子。

QUOTES

關於自己的偶像

"I love Pink and Nelly Furtado—the honesty and truth in their lyrics. I also love Kendrick Lamar and Chance the Rapper."

我喜歡粉紅佳人和妮莉費塔朵，喜歡他們歌詞裡的誠實和真實。我也喜歡肯卓克拉瑪和錢司饒舌。

表演如何融入生活

"My parents never pushed me towards music. I feel like, growing up in a musical household and always being surrounded by it, I was always kind of a performer child. I remember my parents would have guests over, and they would bring their kids, and I would make sure that we were ready to put a show on."

我父母從沒有推著我走音樂的路。我覺得，在一個音樂家庭長大，生活裡都是音樂，向來就是個愛表演的小孩。我記得每當爸媽邀請客人來，他們都會帶小孩，我就確保大家來現場精彩演出。

變得更愛自己

"I'm learning to accept myself. I'm still in the process of learning to love who I am. And it's been really refreshing and really nice to be able to do that and be OK. I think my fans have brought that out in me."

我正在學習接納自己。我正處於學習愛自己的過程。能夠愛自己而且感到自在，真的很舒暢很美好。我覺得是粉絲讓我有所改變。

關於性別歧視

"For a female artist, it takes a lot more to be taken seriously if you're not sat down at a piano or with a guitar, you know?"

你知道嗎？對一個女歌手而言，假如你不是坐在鋼琴前或抱把吉他，你就需要付出更多努力才會被認真看待。

42 向 A 咖西洋歌手學英文

🔊 12 | 名言

關於時尚

"I like how powerful fashion makes me feel. I live for that grungy-prissy juxtaposition that Kate Moss, Naomi Campbell, and Drew Barrymore wore in the '90s."

我喜歡時尚讓我感覺充滿力量。我超愛凱特摩絲、娜歐蜜坎貝兒和茱兒芭莉摩她們九〇年代那種頹廢又矯揉的混搭。

對自己的期許

"Every time you achieve something, you want to go after what's next. I'd like to see my own shows grow and someday be a headliner, fill up stadiums."

每當你達成一項成就，你就想追求下一個目標。我希望看到自己的表演不動成長，有朝一日當主打歌手，體育館塞爆滿。

關於成功

"Success, to me, is just doing things that I'm really proud of."

對我而言，成功就是做這些真正引以為傲的事。

關於心態

"I always told myself never to have a plan B. I feel like that's also one of the reasons I'm doing what I'm doing now, because I just never really rested until I got here."

我總是告訴自己不要留退路。我覺得我現在能做這些事情，這是其中一個原因，我未曾真正停歇才有今天的成就。

© Ben Houdijk / Shutterstock.com

3

STEP 1

掃描書中 QRCode

STEP 2

立即註冊

👤 帳號　限3-21碼小寫英文數字

✉ 信箱

🔒 密碼　限8-24碼小寫英文數字

　　　再次輸入密碼

完成

或

社群帳號註冊

f 使用Facebook註冊

Google　使用Google註冊

快速註冊或登入 EZCourse

STEP 3

回答問題按送出

答案就在書中（需注意空格與大小寫）。

STEP 4

完成訂閱

該書右側會顯示「已訂閱」，表示已成功訂閱，即可點選播放本書音檔。

STEP 5

點選個人檔案

查看「我的訂閱紀錄」會顯示已訂閱本書，點選封面可到本書線上聆聽。

編輯台

對許多英文學習者來說，聽西洋音樂是生活與學習的一部分，編輯我本人就是西洋歌曲愛好者，唱英文歌完全是自發性的跟著歌詞哼唱，唱到不懂的字還會去查，久了也累積不少單字和片語，更別説對聽力和口説更是幫助良多。

書中挑選了 12 位串流平台歌曲下載率最高，以及近期各音樂領域最具代表性的歌手，從對西洋歌手的喜愛做為出發點，報導歌手音樂靈感來源，以及他們的出道契機，介紹成名代表作，如何持續產出好作品以及面對酸民。喜愛西洋歌曲的你可以透過這本書更深入了解歌手，上串流平台聽書中介紹的歌曲，並在文章末閱讀歌手的名言。

書中把歌手分成三類，分類方式依照歌手個人特質與曲風做分類，潮流派歌手的曲風都包含流行樂，較接近朗朗上口的主流音樂。故事型歌手的歌曲和潮流派比起來，情感層次較豐富，彷彿用歌曲説故事。而重砲型歌手，則是因為這些歌手的個性較為直率鮮明，又或是曲風涵蓋搖滾樂，故作此分類。

在英文學習部分，文章難易度符合大考英文閱讀測驗程度，提及的術語與歌手音樂靈感來源都會在 LANGUAGE GUIDE 裡補充説明。除此之外，每篇介紹都使用 4-6 個片語，並在 PHRASES 單元提供用法説明與使用範例，適合教學與自修使用。

除了閱讀以外，你也可透過「聆聽」來學習，只要掃描 QR Code 線上音檔，你就可以聆聽外師朗讀課文、單字、片語範例與名言。最後，不管你使用的音樂載體是串流音樂、CD 光碟，還是近年來又再度走紅的黑膠唱片，祝你在音樂中都能找到自己的真愛、你喜歡的歌手都能大賣。

目次

PART 1 ｜ 潮流派歌手

Justin Bieber
小賈斯汀
你是 Belieber 嗎？

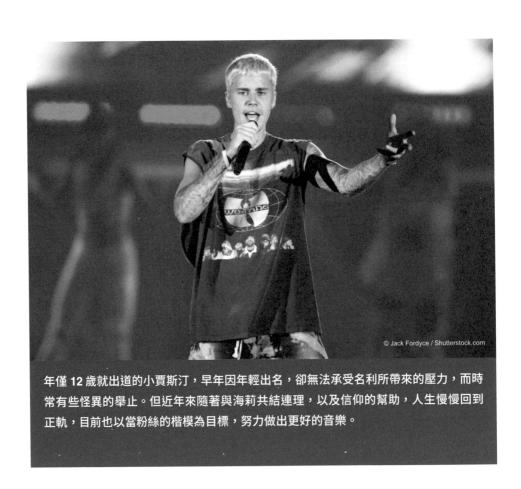

© Jack Fordyce / Shutterstock.com

年僅 12 歲就出道的小賈斯汀，早年因年輕出名，卻無法承受名利所帶來的壓力，而時常有些怪異的舉止。但近年來隨著與海莉共結連理，以及信仰的幫助，人生慢慢回到正軌，目前也以當粉絲的楷模為目標，努力做出更好的音樂。

Love him or hate him, there's no denying that Justin Bieber—known to his millions of ¹⁾**adoring** fans (called Beliebers) as the Biebs, J-Beebs, or simply JB— has been a ²⁾**dominant** force in the music industry for over a decade. And yet he seemed to appear out of nowhere. Born to teenage parents in London and raised by a single mother in the small town of Stratford, both in Ontario—he's Canadian, not British—Bieber grew up poor, although he didn't realize it at the time.

喜歡他也好，討厭他也好，不可否認小賈斯汀叱吒樂壇了十多年。崇拜他的千萬粉絲（叫做 Belieber）稱他為 Biebs 或 J-Beebs，或乾脆只稱 JB。然而他似乎是突然間不知從何處竄起 的。他的爸媽在青少年時期生下了他，他出生於倫敦，而後由單親媽媽撫養，在史特拉福小 鎮長大，倫敦和史特拉福都位於安大略省——他是加拿大人，不是英國人。小賈斯汀出身貧 寒，只不過當時的他並沒有意識到這一點。

His mom liked to ³⁾**blast** pop music on the radio, and she noticed that two- year-old Justin would tap along to the ⁴⁾**rhythm** using any available surface. She couldn't afford music lessons for him, but that's OK. Bieber was a musical *****prodigy**, and over the years taught himself to play not only the drums, but also the piano, trumpet and guitar. He also taught himself how to sing by singing along to ^{LG)}R&B ⁵⁾**hits**, and he got pretty good at it after a while. In 2007, at the age of 12, Bieber sang Ne-Yo's "So Sick" at a Stratford singing ⁶⁾**competition** and placed second.

VOCABULARY

1. adore [əˋdor] (v.) 熱愛，愛慕

2. dominant [ˋdɑmənənt] (a.)
支配的，強勢的

3. blast [blæst] (v.)
（音樂）放很大聲，（喇叭）按很大聲

4. rhythm [ˋrɪðəm] (n.) 節奏，節拍

5. hit [hɪt] (n.) 成功而風行一時的事物

6. competition [ˏkɑmpəˋtɪʃən] (n.)
競賽，競爭

ADVANCED WORDS

*****prodigy** [ˋprɑdədʒɪ] (n.) 天才，奇才

他母親喜歡把收音機裡的流行音樂開得很大聲，她發現兩歲的賈斯汀會跟著音樂節奏敲打手邊任何東西的表面。她無法幫他支付上音樂課的費用，不過沒關係。賈斯汀是音樂天才，幾年下來無師自通學會打鼓，還會鋼琴、小喇叭和吉他。靠著一邊聽節奏藍調名曲一邊跟唱，他也自學了唱歌，最後還唱得很好。2007 年，十二歲的賈斯汀參加了史特拉福當地舉辦的歌唱比賽，選唱尼歐的〈厭倦〉並獲得第二名。

But it's what happened next that ¹⁾**launched** Bieber's career. His mom posted videos of him singing on YouTube, and they quickly <u>**went viral**</u>. When talent manager ^{LG)}**Scooter Braun** saw one of Bieber's videos, he was so impressed by his soulful voice and natural charm that he flew him down to Atlanta to record some songs. Then a chance meeting with ^{LG)}**Usher** led to an ***audition** with the R&B superstar. "His voice was magical and his personality was so keen," said Usher, who signed Bieber to his label and became his ***mentor**—but only after a ²⁾**bidding** war with Justin Timberlake!

接下來發生的事啟動了小賈的音樂事業。媽媽把他唱歌的影片上傳到 YouTube，沒多久就在網路上瘋傳。演藝經紀人史考特布萊恩看到其中一支影片，被他的深情嗓音和個人魅力給深深打動，馬上安排他飛到亞特蘭大錄製歌曲。一次機緣巧合讓他遇到亞瑟小子，獲得在這位節奏藍調天王面前試唱的機會。「他的聲音充滿魔力，個性極為熱心。」亞瑟小子說，並將小賈斯汀簽入自己旗下，成為小賈的導師——但得先經過和賈斯汀提姆布萊克的競標之戰！

VOCABULARY

1. launch [lɔntʃ] (v.) 展開，發表
2. bid [bɪd] (n.) 投標
3. supplement [ˋsʌpləmənt] (v.)
   增加，補充
4. solo [ˋsolo] (a.) 單獨地，單獨的

In the summer of 2009, Bieber dropped his *debut single, "One Time," a teen ^{LG)}pop song about puppy love. It peaked at No. 17 on the ^{LG)}*Billboard* Hot 100, but when the video was released on iTunes, it shot to No. 2—second only to Taylor Swift's "You Belong With Me." This was quickly followed by a seven-track ^{LG)}EP, *My World*, which ³⁾supplemented "One Time" with three other top 40 singles—"One Less Lonely Girl," "Love Me" and "Favorite Girl"—making Bieber the first ⁴⁾solo artist to have four singles in the top 40 before the release of a debut album.

2009 年的夏天，小賈斯汀發行首支單曲〈一生一次〉，是一首描述青澀純愛的青少年流行歌曲。這首歌原在告示牌百大單曲榜排名十七，隨著音樂錄影帶在 iTunes 上面發行而衝上第二，只輸給泰勒絲的〈天生一對〉。他緊接著推出七首歌的迷你專輯《我的全世界》，繼〈一生一次〉之後又有三支單曲打入排行前四十名，分別是〈打敗寂寞〉、〈愛我〉、〈最愛的女孩〉，他也因此成為第一位正規專輯尚未推出就擁有四首排行前四十單曲的獨唱歌手。

ADVANCED WORDS

★ **audition** [ɔˋdɪʃən] (n.)
  試鏡，試演，試唱
★ **mentor** [ˋmɛn͵tɔr] (n.) 精神導師，師父
★ **debut** [ˋde͵bju] (n./v.)
  處女作（指首張專輯，或是每張專輯的首支單曲）

Bieber was already a teen ¹⁾**idol** at this point, but his first full-length album, *My World 2.0*, released in 2010, turned him into an international ²⁾**sensation**. Packed with *****upbeat** teen pop songs like "Baby" and "Somebody to Love," the album debuted at No. 1 on the ^{LG)}***Billboard*** 200 albums chart, making Bieber the youngest singer to top the chart since Stevie Wonder in 1963. He supported the album with his first world tour, singing to stadiums full of screaming Beliebers.

此時小賈斯汀已經成為青少年偶像，但是 2010 年推出的首張正規專輯《我的全世界 2.0》讓他在全球紅翻了天。專輯收錄了〈寶貝〉、〈我愛的人〉等歡快的青少年流行歌曲，空降告示牌二百大專輯榜冠軍，成為繼 1963 年史提夫汪達之後最年輕的冠軍歌手。為了宣傳專輯，他展開生涯第一場世界巡迴演唱會，對著滿場嘶聲尖叫的 Belieber 們演唱他的歌曲。

As Bieber fever swept the ³⁾**globe**, the teen *****heartthrob** could do no wrong. His second studio album, *Under the Mistletoe*, featuring guests like Boyz II Men and Mariah Carey, became the first Christmas album by a male artist to debut at No. 1. As he turned 18, Bieber worked with ⁴⁾**urban** producers to create a more mature dance-⁵⁾**oriented** sound on his next album, *Believe*. Female fans loved his deeper, sexier voice, and imagined he was singing to them on songs like "Boyfriend" and "As Long As You Love Me."

小賈熱潮席捲全球，這位青春萬人迷是不會出錯的。他的第二張錄音室專輯《愛在聖誕》找來大人小孩雙拍檔、瑪麗亞凱莉等跨刀合作，成為第一張由男歌手演唱並空降冠軍的聖誕專輯。隨著小賈斯汀邁入十八歲，他的下一張專輯《我相信》選擇和黑人音樂製作人合作，打

VOCABULARY

1. **idol** [ˈaɪdəl] (n.) 偶像
2. **sensation** [sɛnˈseʃən] (n.)
   轟動（的人事物）
3. **globe** [glob] (n.) 世界，地球
4. **urban** [ˈɝbən] (a.)
   都會的，黑人音樂的
5. **-oriented** [ˈɔriəntɪd] (n.)
   以……為導向的
6. **fame** [fem] (n.) 聲望，名聲
7. **behavior** [bɪˈhevjɚ] (n.) 行為，舉止
8. **abandon** [əˈbændən] (v.) 丟棄，遺棄
9. **mansion** [ˈmænʃən] (n.) 豪宅

造更為成熟的舞曲導向聲音。女粉絲們愛他更低沉、性感的嗓音，想像他正對著自己唱〈男朋友〉、〈只要你愛我〉這些歌。

But it wasn't all **smooth sailing** for the Biebs. Perhaps due to the pressures of achieving wealth and ⁶⁾**fame**, especially at such a young age, the young singer began to go out of control. It started with odd ⁷⁾**behavior**, like ⁸⁾**abandoning** his pet monkey in Germany and peeing in a restaurant mop bucket. But then he began breaking the law, throwing eggs at his neighbor's ⁹⁾**mansion** in California, and, more seriously, **driving under the influence** and resisting arrest at an *****illegal** street race in Miami.

但是小賈的生涯並非一帆風順。或許因為名利帶來的壓力，尤其在尚未成熟的年紀，這位年輕歌手開始失控暴走。先是出現怪異行為，像是把寵物猴丟在德國、在餐廳的拖把水桶裡小便。然後開始做一些違法的事，朝加州鄰居豪宅扔雞蛋，更嚴重的是他酒後在邁阿密街頭飆車並且拒捕。

Bieber's fans remained ¹⁰⁾**loyal**, however, and it wasn't long before he made a *****comeback**. In 2015, he explored ᴸᴳ⁾**EDM** on the hit song "Where Are Ü Now," a ¹¹⁾**collaboration** with Skrillex and Diplo that won him the ᴸᴳ⁾**Grammy** for Best Dance Recording. This led to his next album, *Purpose*, a collection of EDM and dance-pop songs with more personal themes, like "Love Yourself" and "Sorry"—widely seen as an ¹²⁾**apology** to his **on-again, off-again** girlfriend, actress and singer Selena Gomez.

VOCABULARY	ADVANCED WORDS
10. loyal [ˈlɔɪəl] (a.) 忠誠的，忠心的 **11. collaboration** [kəˌlæbəˈreʃən] (n.) 　　合作，協作，動詞為 　　**collaborate** [kəˈlæbəˌret] **12. apology** [əˈpɑlədʒi] (n.) 道歉，賠罪	＊**upbeat** [ˈʌpˌbit] (a.) 樂觀的，歡快的 ＊**heartthrob** [ˈhɑrtˌθrɑb] (n.) 迷戀的對象 ＊**illegal** [ɪˈligəl] (a.) 不合法的 ＊**comeback** [ˈkʌmˌbæk] (n.) 　　復出，東山再起

小賈的粉絲死忠依舊，過沒多久他就捲土重來。2015 年，他和史奇雷克斯與迪波洛聯手打造熱門歌曲〈你在哪裡〉，嘗試電子舞曲風格，為他贏得葛萊美獎的最佳舞曲錄音。下一張專輯《我的決心》延續前作，混和了電子舞曲和流行舞曲，並探討更為私人的主題，像是〈愛你自己〉和〈對不起〉──後者普遍被認為是他唱給分分合合的女友、演員兼歌手賽琳娜的道歉之作。

Since then, Bieber has kept growing—as an artist, and as a person. Further collaborations have taken him in new musical directions: like his vocals on Luis Fonsi's "Despacito," which won him a *Latin Grammy. He's also settled down and become a responsible adult, marrying model Hailey Baldwin and getting [1]involved in social *justice* [2]issues. This new focus is [3]evident on his 2021 album Justice, which includes quotes from civil rights leader Dr. Martin Luther King, Jr. "In a time when there's so much wrong with this broken planet," says Bieber, "we all *crave healing and justice for [4]humanity." Are you a Belieber?

此後小賈斯汀無論作為歌手或個人都不斷成長。接下來的音樂合作讓他朝新的音樂方向發展：他在路易斯馮西的歌曲〈慢慢來〉中獻聲，為他拿下一座拉丁葛萊美獎。他也終於安頓下來，成為一個負責任的大人，與模特兒海莉鮑德溫結婚，參與社會正義問題。2021 年發行的專輯《我的正義》展現了小賈的新視野，當中引用了民權領袖金恩博士的一些話語。小賈說：「在這破碎星球百弊叢生的時代，我們都渴望人類獲得治癒，正義得以伸張。」你是否也是相信小賈的 Belieber 呢？

VOCABULARY

1. **involve** [ɪn`vɑlvd] (v.) 致力於，涉入
2. **issue** [`ɪʃju] (n.) 議題，問題
3. **evident** [`ɛvɪdənt] (a.) 明顯的，明白的
4. **humanity** [hju`mænəti] (n.)
   人類，人道

ADVANCED WORDS

* **Latin** [`lætɪn] (a.)
   拉丁美洲的，拉丁美洲人的
* **crave** [krev] (v.) 渴望

LANGUAGE GUIDE (LG)

R&B 節奏藍調

全名為 rhythm and blues。除了保有藍調音樂的形式，還融入爵士樂和福音音樂的風格，後來再發展出放克音樂、靈魂樂、搖滾樂等多種音樂類型。

Scooter Braun 史考特布萊恩

美國企業家與亞莉安娜、肯伊威斯特、小賈斯汀等歌手的經紀人，於 2019 年 6 月宣布收購泰勒絲的前唱片公司大機器唱片，並取得泰勒絲前 6 張專輯的版權，引發不滿。

Usher 亞瑟小子

出生於 1978 年，為美國 R&B 歌手，至今發行過 10 張專輯，曾獲 8 座葛萊美獎，2004 年單曲「Yeah!」連續 12 周在告示牌百大單曲榜上第一。

pop 流行音樂

為流行音樂的一種類型，為 popular music「流行音樂」的縮寫，吸引廣大聽眾，歌詞主題常為生活與愛情。流行樂也有分支，例如電子流行、合成器流行、流行舞曲等。

Billboard Hot 100 告示牌百大單曲榜 / *Billboard* 200 告示牌二百大專輯榜

告示牌榜單展示了單曲或專輯在美國及其他地方的受歡迎程度，每期榜單都會刊載在《告示牌》(*Billboard*) 雜誌上。告示牌百大單曲榜根據唱片銷售量、電台點播量或串流媒體在線播放量來制訂。對於告示牌二百大專輯榜，無論是實體唱片，還是整張數位專輯及串流專輯的銷量，都計算在專輯銷量內。

EP 迷你專輯

台灣多把 EP 稱為「單曲專輯」，其實 EP 是介於單曲 (single) 和專輯之間的作品，收錄四到八首歌曲。相較於 EP，LP（又稱為 full-length）就是所謂的「專輯唱片」，有十首歌以上。歌手除了發行專輯，還會發行單曲 (single)，指包含一首歌曲或相對於專輯歌曲中比較簡短的版本。

EDM 電子舞曲

全名為 electronic dance music，是用電子合成器，電子鼓，或用現有唱片音樂片段融合而成的一種音樂。經常在夜店播放，其特點是強烈的舞曲節奏。

Grammy 葛萊美獎

葛萊美獎 (Grammy Awards) 是美國音樂界最重要的獎項之一，由錄音學院 (Recording Academy) 頒發，和告示牌音樂獎和全美音樂獎 (American Music Awards) 共稱作「三大（獎）」(the Big Three)。

PHRASES

go viral 網路爆紅

viral 表示「如病毒般快速的（傳播）」，表示透過社群媒體在網路上快速與廣泛的傳播，迅速獲得專注與宣傳。

A Did that video of your cat end up **going viral**?
你的貓咪影片在網路上爆紅了嗎？

B Yeah. It has over two million views.
對，已經有兩百萬次點閱了。

smooth sailing 一帆風順

也可以說 clear sailing。sail 當動詞是「航行」的意思，既然用 smooth（順利的、平穩的）來形容這個航行，當然就是一帆風順，拿來描述事情進行得很順利。

A How did your exam go this morning?
你早上的考試如何？

B The essay questions were kind of hard, but the rest was **smooth sailing**.
申論題有點難，但是其他部分都還蠻順利的。

driving under the influence (DUI) 在醉酒或吸毒後駕駛

這裡的 influence（影響）指的是受到酒精或是毒品或藥物的影響。駕駛在飲酒或服用藥物後，會影響安全駕駛能力。不但是交通違規行為，也可算是犯罪行為。

A Why did Kevin have his license suspended?
凱文為什麼被吊銷駕照？

B He was arrested for **driving under the influence**.
他因涉嫌酒後駕車被捕。

on-again, off-again 分分合合

想形容情侶分手又復合的反覆愛情關係，就可以在 on（進行的）和 off（結束的）後面直接加上 again 來表示。

A Did you hear Jill and Pete got back together?

你有聽說吉兒和彼特又復合了嗎？

B I'm not surprised. They've been in an **on-again, off-again** relationship for years.

我不訝異。他們兩個分分合合好幾年了。

▲ 小賈和賽琳娜在 2011 年至 2018 年間交往約 8 年時間，期間兩人多次分分合合，分手後不久即和現任妻子海莉閃婚。

QUOTES

談到討厭他的人

"Of course, I think that people are just waiting for that time when I make a mistake and they're gonna jump on it.... There's gonna be haters."

當然，我覺得大家只是在等我犯錯然後大肆批評……就是會有討厭你的人。

談到自己對信仰的態度

"You don't need to go to church to be a Christian. If you go to Taco Bell, that doesn't make you a taco."

不是一定要上教堂才是基督徒，你去塔可鐘（Taco Bell 為知名塔可餐廳）也不會變成塔可餅啊。

談起自身性格

"I grew up below the poverty line; I didn't have as much as other people did. I think it made me stronger as a person; it built my character."

我是窮著長大的，我擁有的沒有別人多。我認為那塑造了我的性格，讓我成為更堅強的人。

對於名氣的看法

"When you've reached a certain point in your life, there are people out there waiting to see you fall. But rather than let gravity take you down, sometimes you have to take matters into your own hands and fly."

當你達到人生的某個高峰，就會有人等著看你跌落。與其任憑重力帶你下墜，有時你必須掌握自己命運、奮力飛翔。

談到自己的人生

"I'm living proof that dreams do come true. Work hard. Pray. Believe."

我就是夢想會成真的活生生證明。努力。祈禱。相信。

關於恩師亞瑟小子

"When I hear him sing and see what he can do, though, it's always a reminder of why I look up to Usher as my mentor and why I will always be an Usher fan to my core. But I'm lucky to say that he's an even better friend to me than he's a mentor. He's truly the real deal."

每當我聽亞瑟小子唱歌、看到他的本事，總會記得自己為何視他如師，為何永遠都會是他的鐵粉。但我可以很幸運地說，比起做我的導師，他是我更好的朋友。他真的不是蓋的。

現在的目標

"Young people in the business have grown up and made the wrong decisions, or bad decisions, and haven't been good role models. To be someone that people look up to is important to me."

演藝界的年輕人長大了、做了錯誤的決定或不好的決定，沒能成為好榜樣。成為令人尊敬的人對我來說很重要。

對年輕人的勉勵

"Be humble, be grateful, give back, share, pay it forward, chase your dreams, go for it, and take a moment to remember where it is all from."

要謙卑、感恩、回饋、分享，把愛傳出去，勇敢追夢，放手一搏，更不要忘記你所擁有的一切從何而來。

Ariana Grande
亞莉安娜格蘭德

嗓音宏亮的嬌小歌姬

© Tinseltown / Shutterstock.com

亞莉安娜以其甜美的高馬尾形象,以及寬廣音域而著名。事實上她個人生活的精采程度,絲毫不亞於她的歌曲。和歷任男友轟轟烈烈的戀情,曾經讓她背負劈腿罵名,又或是在新一任男友尚未離婚前,就正式開始交往。可說是敢愛敢恨,無畏他人眼光的新女性。

The Tiny Diva with the Big Voice

Ariana Grande, the 5-foot-tall pop ^LG)diva with the huge four-^LG)octave ^1)vocal range, was born into an Italian-American family in Boca Raton, Florida on June, 26, 1993. Although her parents are both successful in business—her mom, Joan, is *CEO of a family company, and her dad, Edward, runs his own ^2)graphic design firm—^3)entertaining <u>runs in the family</u>. Ariana's brother Frankie, who is 10 years older than her, is a Broadway ^4)performer who has appeared in hit musicals like *Rock of Ages* and *Mamma Mia!* "Once Frankie got into acting in musical theater and dancing," she says, "I was like, 'OK, I guess that's the cool thing now.'"

亞莉安娜格蘭德是一名流行歌姬，1993 年 6 月 26 日出生於佛州博卡拉頓的一個義大利裔美國人家庭，身高只有 153 公分，音域卻可跨四個八度音階。她的父母經商事業有成——母親瓊恩是家族企業的執行長，父親愛德華經營自己的平面設計公司——然而表演可是家族共通的天分。大她十歲的哥哥法蘭基是百老匯演員，曾參與知名音樂劇如《搖滾時代》、《媽媽咪呀！》。「法蘭基成為音樂劇演員和一名舞者時，」亞莉安娜說，「我就想：『好欸，這才酷啊。』

VOCABULARY

1. **vocal** [vokəl] (a./n.) 聲的，歌唱的；歌唱（表演），**vocal range** 即「音域」
2. **graphic** [ˋɡræfɪk] (a.) 圖解的，圖畫的
3. **entertain** [ˌɛntəˋten] (v.) 娛樂，表演
4. **performer** [pəˋfɔrmə] (n.) 表演者，演奏者

ADVANCED WORDS

* **CEO** [ˋsi ˋi ˋo] (abbr.) 執行長，即 **chief executive officer** 的縮寫

But it was Ariana's mom who first realized she could sing. One day in the car when she was just three or four, Joan was amazed to find that she was hitting all the high notes in an NSYNC song on the radio. Ariana soon became the star on family *karaoke nights. "The [1]soundtrack was Whitney, Madonna, Mariah, Celine, Barbra," says Joan. "All the divas." She later **followed in Frankie's footsteps**, performing in local theater [2]productions of *Annie*, *The Wizard of Oz* and *Beauty and the Beast*. And at age 15, Ariana landed the role of *cheerleader Charlotte in the Broadway musical *13*, for which she won a National Youth Theater [3]Association Award.

最早發現亞莉安娜會唱歌的是她的母親。有一天母親開車載著才三、四歲的她,收音機正播放著超級男孩的歌曲,而亞莉安娜竟然能夠精準地飆唱每個高音,令瓊恩大吃一驚。沒多久,亞莉安娜就成為家庭 K 歌之夜的明星。「她唱的都是惠妮休斯頓、瑪丹娜、瑪麗亞凱莉、席琳狄翁、芭芭拉史翠珊,」瓊恩說,「都是知名歌姬。」後來她跟隨法蘭基的腳步,參與社區劇院的一些歌舞劇表演如《安妮》、《綠野仙蹤》和《美女與野獸》。亞莉安娜十五歲時演出百老匯音樂劇《13》中的啦啦隊長夏綠蒂一角,並以此榮獲國家青年戲劇協會獎。

Now that she was in the national [4]spotlight, Ariana was invited to audition for *Victorious*, a Nickelodeon teen *sitcom about a group of students at a performing arts high school in Hollywood. She won the role of Cat, a sweet but [5]naïve teen with bright red hair—she damaged her hair from [6]dying it so much—that quickly became a fan favorite. The role turned Ariana into a TV star, but she wanted to be a singer. "I hate acting," she says. "It's fun, but music has always been **first and foremost** with me."

VOCABULARY

1. **soundtrack** [ˈsaʊndˌtræk] (n.)
   電影原聲帶（電影中使用的歌曲）
2. **production** [prəˈdʌkˌʃən] (n.)
   戲劇演出
3. **association** [əˌsosiˈeʃən] (n.)
   協會,聯盟

4. **spotlight** [ˈspɑtˌlaɪt] (n.)
   聚光燈,公眾注意的中心
5. **naïve** [nɑˈiv] (a.) 天真的,幼稚的
6. **dye** [daɪ] (v./n.) 染色；染料
7. **upload** (v.) [ˈʌpˌlod]（電腦）上傳
8. **certify** [ˈsɜtəˌfaɪ] (v.) 核證,頒發

既然她站上了全國舞台，便受邀參加尼克兒童頻道的青少年情境喜劇《勝利之歌》的試鏡，這齣劇講述好萊塢一間表演藝術高中裡面一群學生的故事。她獲得了凱特這個角色，一名有著豔紅頭髮、個性傻萌的可愛少女，為了演出此角她染髮過度，髮質都壞了，卻迅速成為粉絲的最愛。這個角色讓亞莉安娜當上電視明星，但是她真正想當的是歌手。「我不喜歡演戲，」她說，「演戲很有趣，但音樂對我而言才是最重要的。」

So while she continued playing Cat in *Victorious*, Ariana worked with a vocal coach to strengthen her voice and began [7]**uploading** videos of herself singing Adele, Whitney Houston and Mariah Carey *covers to YouTube. **Blown away** by her vocals in the videos, the CEO of Republic Records gave her a record deal, and she started working on her debut album. In December 2011, Ariana released her first single, "Put Your Hearts Up," a *bubblegum pop song aimed at young Cat fans. But even though the song was eventually [8]**certified** gold, she said it's "just not my *vibe," and decided she wanted her album to sound like the '90s R&B she listened to growing up.

於是，亞莉安娜一邊繼續演出《勝利之歌》中的凱特，一邊請來聲樂教師加強她的聲音，並開始將她翻唱愛黛兒、惠妮休斯頓、瑪麗亞凱莉等歌手的影片上傳到 YouTube。聯眾唱片的執行長聽了她的歌聲驚為天人，提出一紙唱片合約，於是她就開始籌備首張專輯了。2011 年 12 月，亞莉安娜發行第一支單曲〈捧起你的心〉，是一首針對年輕的凱特粉絲而打造的泡泡糖流行歌曲。雖然這首歌最終獲得黃金認證，她卻表示這「不是我的調調」，她希望專輯走的是陪伴她長大的九〇年代節奏藍調風格。

ADVANCED WORDS

* **karaoke** [ˌkɛrɪˋoki] (n.) 卡拉 OK
* **cheerleader** [ˋtʃɪrˌlidə] (n.) 啦啦隊員
* **sitcom** [ˋsɪtˌkɑm] (n.) 情境喜劇，即 **situation comedy** 的縮寫
* **cover** [ˋkʌvə] (n./v.) 翻唱，指將原歌曲改由他人以另一種方式重新詮釋

* **bubblegum** [ˋbʌbəlˌgʌm] (a.) 符合年輕人喜好的
* **vibe** [vaɪb] (n.) 氣氛，給人的感覺

And it's a good thing she followed her [1])**instincts**. When *Yours Truly* was finally released in 2013, it debuted at No. 1 on the *Billboard* 200 chart. Featuring singles like "The Way," a collaboration with [LG)]**rapper** [LG)]**Mac Miller** that became her first top ten hit, the album *****showcased** Ariana's impressive vocal range and ability to combine pop, R&B, and [LG)]**hip hop** influences, [2)]**establishing** her as a rising star. And her *****winning streak** continued in 2014 with *My Everything*, which also debuted on top of the *Billboard* 200. Adding EDM to Ariana's pop and R&B [3)]**formula**, the album produced four top ten hits—including "Problem" with Iggy Azalea and "Love Me Harder" with The Weeknd—the most of any artist that year.

好在她聽從了自己的直覺，終於在 2013 年發行了專輯《真情歌》，並空降告示牌二百大榜首。專輯收錄了和饒舌歌手麥克米勒合作的〈愛你的方式〉，是她首支排行前十的單曲。而這張專輯展現了亞莉安娜驚人的音域，以及融合流行、節奏藍調和嘻哈元素的能力，確立了她明日之星的地位。2014 年推出的專輯《我的全部》再次空降告示牌二百大榜首，締造了連勝佳績。在這張專輯中，亞莉安娜在其一貫的流行和節奏藍調中加入電子舞曲風，創造出四首排行前十的熱門歌曲，包括和伊姬阿潔莉亞合唱的〈愛情麻煩〉，還有和威肯合作的〈用力愛我〉，是當年最多首歌曲闖進前十的歌手。

Now that Ariana was a pop superstar, she went for a darker, sexier, more mature sound on her next album, *Dangerous Woman*, released in 2016. With top ten hits like "Side to Side" featuring Nicki Minaj and the *****sultry** "Dangerous Woman," it helped her win Artist of the Year at the [LG)]**American Music Awards**. During the Dangerous Woman Tour in 2017, however, [4)]**tragedy** struck. A bomb attack at

---

VOCABULARY

1. **instinct** [ˈɪnstɪŋkt] (n.) 本能，直覺
2. **establish** [ɪˈstæblɪʃ] (v.) 確立（某種地位）
3. **formula** [ˈfɔrmjələ] (n.) 配方，公式，方法
4. **tragedy** [ˈtrædʒədi] (n.) 悲劇
5. **trauma** [ˈtrɔmə] (n.)（精神）創傷
6. **overcome** [ˌovɚˈkʌm] (v.) 克服，戰勝
7. **inspiration** [ˌɪnspəˈreʃən] (n.) 靈感
8. **celebration** [ˌsɛləˈbreʃən] (n.) 慶祝活動，慶典

her concert in Manchester, England claimed the lives of 22 people and injured hundreds. Ariana responded by organizing the One Love Manchester benefit concert, which raised millions for the victims and their families.

既然亞莉安娜已經躋身流行巨星，在 2016 年發行的下一張專輯《危險尤物》中，她開始嘗試一種更陰暗、性感和成熟的聲音。專輯打進排名前十的單曲包括邀來妮姬米娜合作演唱的〈招搖〉，以及撩撥春心的〈危險尤物〉，也為她贏得全美音樂獎的年度藝人大獎。然而就在 2017 年的危險尤物巡演途中，發生了一起悲劇。她在英國曼徹斯特舉行的演唱會遭到炸彈攻擊，造成二十二人喪命，數百人受傷。亞莉安娜做出了正面的回應，舉辦了《曼徹斯特齊心獻愛》慈善演唱會，將募得的數百萬款項捐給受害者和其家屬。

The bomb attack <u>took a toll</u> on Ariana's mental health, and she naturally turned to music to help her process the 5)**trauma**. On 2018's *Sweetener*, which won a Grammy for Best Pop Vocal Album, lead single "No Tears Left to Cry" is an optimistic song on 6)**overcoming** tragedy, and "Breathin'" is about how she used deep breathing to deal with ***panic attacks**. For her next album, *Thank U, Next*, Ariana drew 7)**inspiration** from a different kind of trauma—failed relationships. In the title track, she sings about getting over, among others, actor LG)**Pete Davidson**, who she almost married, and Mac Miller, who died of an ***overdose** after their two-year relationship ended. Both "Thank U, Next" and "7 Rings"—a LG)**trap** 8)**celebration** of material success—debuted at No. 1 on the Hot 100.

ADVANCED WORDS

* **showcase** [ˈʃoˌkes] (v.)
   展示
* **winning streak** [ˈwɪnɪŋ strik] (n.)
   接連獲勝
* **sultry** [ˈsʌltrɪ] (a.)
   性感撩人的，風情萬種的

* **panic attack** [ˈpænɪk əˈtæk] (n.)
   恐慌發作
* **overdose** [ˈovɚˌdos] (n.)
   吸毒、服藥過量

炸彈攻擊事件讓亞莉安娜心理蒙上陰影，為了療癒創傷，她自然而然投入音樂的懷抱。2018 年發行的專輯《甜到翻》奪下葛萊美獎最佳流行演唱專輯，首發單曲〈淚已流乾〉以積極樂觀的態度描述如何克服悲劇，〈呼吸〉則描述她如何運用深呼吸度過恐慌發作。接著發行的專輯《謝謝，下一位》則是從另一種類型的創傷——感情失敗——中汲取靈感。她在專輯的同名歌曲中談到過去種種關係，唱到分手後如何忘記已論及婚嫁的演員男友彼特戴維斯，以及結束兩年戀情後因藥物過量而殞命的麥克米勒。這首〈謝謝，下一位〉和慶祝物質生活富裕的陷阱音樂歌曲〈七枚鑽戒〉都在告示牌百大熱門排行榜上空降冠軍。

Speaking of No. 1 debuts, Ariana broke the record for the most No. 1 debuts in Hot 100 history with the title track of her R&B-heavy sixth album, *Positions*. Not only that, all 14 tracks on *Positions* charted on the Hot 100 [1]**simultaneously**. How many pop divas can **pull that off**? And now, after a break to film the screen [2]**adaptation** of *Wicked*, she's just released her seventh album, *Eternal Sunshine*.

說到空降冠軍，亞莉安娜可是以其第六張專輯、走濃厚節奏藍調風的《性感到位》同名主打歌，創下最多支空降冠軍單曲的紀錄。不僅如此，《性感到位》中的十四首歌曲甚至同時登上告示牌百大單曲榜。有多少流行歌姬做得到？而此時，因投入螢幕改編作品《魔法壞女巫》的拍攝而短暫暌違樂壇之後，亞莉安娜才剛剛發行了第七張專輯《永恆陽光》。

VOCABULARY

1. **simultaneously.** [ˌsaɪməlˋteniəsli]
   (adv.) 同時地
2. **adaptation** [ˌædæpˋteʃən] (n.)
   改編，改寫

LANGUAGE GUIDE (LG)

diva 歌后

拉丁文中「女神」的意思，常被用來指稱在戲劇和音樂領域具有傑出才華的知名女性。也可以指以喜怒無常或嚴格要求而聞名的女藝人，像是瑪麗亞凱莉和瑪丹娜就有終極天后 (ultimate diva) 之稱。

octave 八度

是音程的一種，為相鄰音組中相同音名的兩個音。一般人的音域大約一個半八度，其他可跨四個八度音階的歌手還有克里絲汀阿奎萊拉、碧昂絲、馬文蓋，知名天后瑪麗亞凱莉的歌聲可跨越 5 個八度。

rap / rapper 饒舌（歌手）

一種帶有節奏和押韻 (rhyme) 的說唱方式，歌詞充滿自誇驕傲的氣氛，配上重複性強的節拍，與嘻哈文化關係密切。rapper 為「饒舌歌手」。饒舌發源於七〇年代的紐約，Jay-Z 和 Kanye West 為目前當紅饒舌歌手的表率。

Mac Miller 麥克米勒

美國饒舌歌手與唱片製作人。2016 年 8 月，他開始和亞莉安娜交往，在 2018 年五月分手。在 2018 年 9 月 7 日因藥物過量而於家中昏迷，搶救後不治而離世，享年 26 歲。

Hip-Hop Music 嘻哈音樂

是一種跟著伴奏、帶著韻律吟誦即饒舌的音樂風格。起源自七〇年代美國內陸城市的非裔青少年，及紐約市拉丁美洲裔青少年。饒舌音樂 (rap) 也是嘻哈的一種。

American Music Awards 全美音樂獎

1973 年，為了與葛萊美獎競爭，迪克克拉克 (Dick Clark) 創辦全美音樂獎。該獎項得主由唱片消費者票選決定，沒有設置最佳單曲與最佳唱片的獎項。

Pete Davidson 彼得戴維森

為美國喜劇演員，在 2014 年至 2022 年間為美國知名喜劇節目《週六夜現場》的固定班底。和亞莉安娜交往 5 個月後，兩人取消婚約、分手。他也曾和金卡戴珊、凱特貝琴薩，以及飾演《女傭浮生錄》的瑪格麗特庫利交往。

trap music 陷阱音樂

Trap 是嘻哈音樂的一個子流派，起源於美國南部，得名於亞特蘭大俚語 trap house（陷阱屋），專門用來販賣毒品的房子。使用合成鼓、踩鈸等樂器，創造出陰暗、詭異、迷幻的氛圍。

PHRASES

(sth.) runs in the family 世代相傳、家族遺傳

如果某種特質、能力、疾病在不同世代的家族裡流傳，表示家庭成員經常表現出的特徵，或是遺傳特徵。

A Wow, Michael is so handsome.
   哇，麥可還真帥。

B So is his dad. Good looks **run in the family**.
   他爸爸也是，好看的基因在這家族世代相傳。

follow in sb.'s footsteps 步某人後塵，效法某人

footstep 顧名思義即為「腳步，步伐」，而 follow in sb.'s footsteps 就是追隨某人的腳步、步上某人的後塵。

A You're going to art school? I thought your dad wanted you to study medicine.
   你要去讀美術？你老爸不是要你去念醫科。

B Yeah, but I don't want to **follow in his footsteps**.
   是沒錯，但我不想要跟他走一樣的路。

first and foremost 首要的是，最重要的

foremost 表示「最前面的，最先的」，和 first 意思相同，兩個字合在一起即表示「首要的，重要的」。

A Why did you decide to turn down the job offer?
   你為什麼決定回絕這份工作？

B **First and foremost**, the pay is too low.
   主要是因為薪水太低。

blow (sb.) away 令人大開眼界

blow sb. away 就是「使某人驚嘆不已，令某人大為驚奇」，而 sb. be blown away by sth. 即表示「某人對⋯⋯極為著迷」或「⋯⋯使某人印象極為深刻、大受感動」。

A I was **blown away** by the Picasso exhibition.
畢卡索展讓我嘆為觀止。

B I thought it was good, but not that good.
我覺得是不錯啦，但沒那麼好。

take a toll (on) 對⋯⋯造成負面影響

toll 是「損害」的意思。take a toll 或 take its/their toll 是「造成負面影響」，後面介系詞常用 on。

A I can't believe Rachael is only 30—she looks 40 at least.
真不敢相信瑞秋只有三十歲──她看起來至少四十了。

B I know. All those years of sunbathing have really **taken a toll on** her skin.
對啊。多年來狂做日光浴真的很傷她的皮膚。

pull (sth.) off 成功，圓滿完成

pull sth. off 或 pull it/that off 是「努力實現」的意思，通常是在困難的情況下，依然能夠圓滿達到目標。

A Did you hear that Jason passed the bar exam?
你聽說傑森通過律師資格考試了嗎？

B No. I'm impressed. I didn't think he could **pull it off**.
沒有，我真佩服。我沒想到他會通過。

QUOTES

談論交往對象

"I've done the bad boy thing. It was fun for a good three months. But the thing about bad boys is, you have to keep in mind, you're never gonna marry a bad boy."

我也交往過壞男孩，前三個月的確過得很開心。不過關於壞男孩，有件事你一定要記住，你永遠不會嫁給壞男孩。

談論嗜好

"I just love to shop. If I could, I would shop every single day in every single store and spend all of my money which, you know, I do anyway."

我就是愛血拼。如果可以，我會每天血拼，買遍所有商店，把錢花光光。總之我是把錢都拿去血拼了。

談論厭女情結

"Misogyny is ever-present, and we have to be there to support one another. That's really it. It's about the sisterhood. There's no competing in that. We have to lift each other up, not try and claw each other down."

厭女情結一直存在，我們必須互相扶持，真的。姊妹們一定要相挺，沒有競爭的。我們要彼此支持而不是把對方扯下。

談論曼徹斯特恐怖攻擊

"I don't think we've ever been through anything as traumatic as what we've been through."

我認為這次經歷的創傷是過去所有經歷都無法比擬的。

談論網路霸凌

"I can't stress to you enough how much I can relate to teens being cyberbullied. Something that helps me is looking at old videos of me and my friends from middle school, or videos of my family. I love watching funny videos of my favorite people--It really cheers me up."

我真的必須說我能體會青少年被網路霸凌的滋味。這種時候我會看一些以前自己和國中同學的影片，或者看家人的影片，對我很有幫助。我喜歡看我愛的人的有趣影片，總是能讓我開心起來。

身心平衡的方法

"Meditation is a great way to keep my body well-centered while juggling shooting schedules and recording sessions."

當我得同時兼顧拍攝行程和錄音活動時，冥想是讓身體維持平衡的一個好方式。

自己的偶像

"I'm a big perfectionist! I'm trying to channel super-confident women like Alicia Keys, Mariah Carey and Beyoncé, because I realized that if you want something, you really have to go for it, just like they do."

我是超級完美主義者！我想要跟隨那些超級自信的女性，像是艾莉西亞凱斯、瑪麗亞凱莉和碧昂絲，因為我發現如果你想要一樣東西，就必須自己去爭取，像她們一樣。

Dua Lipa
杜娃黎波
從家鄉科索沃邁向國際知名歌手

© ako photography / shutterstock.com

杜娃黎波出生於 1995 年，為英國及阿爾巴尼亞的創作歌手，曲風為流行、迪斯可等，以其低沉渾厚的嗓音，以及亮麗的外型在流行樂壇佔有一席之地。她也善用自己的影響力為少數族群發聲，十分有勇氣。

From Kosovo to Global Pop Sensation

They say **the apple doesn't fall far from the tree**, and that's ¹⁾**definitely** true of Dua Lipa. Her father had enjoyed success as the ^{LG)}**lead vocalist** of ^{LG)}**rock band** Oda in his native ^{LG)}**Kosovo**. In addition to ***honing** his ²⁾**craft** at home, he played CDs featuring songs by ³⁾**legendary** artists like Bob Dylan, David Bowie and Radiohead. Growing up in this environment, it seemed natural that Dua Lipa would **follow suit**.

有其父必有其女,這句話用來形容杜娃黎波再貼切不過了。他父親曾是搖滾樂團 Oda 的主唱,在家鄉科索沃小有名氣。平常在家除了精進歌藝也會播放 CD 唱片,聽一些傳奇歌手如巴布狄倫、大衛鮑伊和電台司令的歌。耳濡目染之下,杜娃黎波跟隨父親的腳步似乎是很自然的事。

By the age of six, Dua Lipa was already showing a gift for performance, singing along to her favorite songs. She ⁴⁾**cites** singer ^{LG)}**Pink** as a major influence. Yet Lipa's dreams suffered an early ***blow** while she was a primary school student in London. While auditioning for the school ⁵⁾**choir**, she was told by music teachers that her voice was too low to hit the high notes. In fact, the teachers went further, saying the young student lacked the talent to be a singer.

杜娃黎波六歲時就展現出表演能力,能夠跟著自己最愛的音樂哼唱。她提到自己深受粉紅佳人影響。然而她的夢想在小時候就遭到打擊,那時她在倫敦念小學。她參加學校合唱團的徵選,音樂老師說她的聲線太低了,唱不了高音。事實上,老師還說這位年幼學生沒有當歌手的天賦。

VOCABULARY

1. **definitely** [ˋdɛfənɪtlɪ] (adv.) 一定地,絕對地
2. **craft** [kræft] (n.) 才藝
3. **legendary** [ˋlɛdʒən͵dɛrɪ] (a.) 傳說中的,著名的
4. **cite** [saɪt] (v.) 舉例,引用
5. **choir** [kwaɪr] (n.) 合唱團,唱詩班

ADVANCED WORDS

* **hone** [hon] (v.) 磨練
* **blow** [blo] (n.) 打擊

Fifteen years later, those *naysayers have egg on their faces. Ignoring their
1)criticism, Dua Lipa has achieved international *superstardom. In fact, her
deep voice has become her 2)trademark.

十五年後，那些唱衰她的人如今顏面盡失。杜娃黎波無視他們的批評，成為國際超級巨星。
事實上，她那低沉渾厚的嗓音反倒成了她的註冊商標。

It's not surprising that Lipa was able to overcome these problems, given the
3)determination she showed from a young age. In 2008, her parents returned
to their birthplace, Pristina, the capital of Kosovo. The country had just gained
independence after a bloody war. Although her family wasn't affected by the
violence personally, she has classmates who suffered. Yet she found Pristina
"way safer" than London, and remembers her time there fondly. Her LG)Albanian
improved, she learned about LG)Kosovar culture, and she made close friends.
When hip hop stars like Snoop Dogg and 50 Cent performed in Pristina, Lipa was
able to attend their concerts, thanks to her father's connections.

黎波小小年紀就展現決心，克服這些問題並不令人意外。2008 年，她的父母搬回出生地、
科索沃的首都普里斯提納居住。科索沃才剛經歷一場血戰取得獨立。雖然她家並沒有受到暴
力事件影響，卻有同學蒙受苦難。儘管如此，她還是覺得普里斯提納比倫敦「安全得多」，
深深懷念那裡的時光。她的阿爾巴尼亞語進步了（阿爾巴尼亞語為科索沃的官方語言之
一），也認識了科索沃文化，交了一些好朋友。當史努比狗狗和五角這些嘻哈歌手到普里斯
提納演出時，她也靠著父親的關係得以聽到他們的演唱會。

VOCABULARY

1. **criticism** (n.) [ˈkrɪtəˌsɪzəm]
   批評，評論

2. **trademark** [ˈtredˌmɑrk] (n.)
   招牌，代表性物品

3. **determination** [dɪˌtɜməˈneʃən] (n.)
   堅毅，決心

4. **career** [kəˈrɪr] (n.) 職業，生涯

5. **enroll** [ɪnˈrol] (v.)（註冊）入學

6. **website** [ˈwɛbˌsaɪt] (n.)
   （電腦）網站

7. **agency** [ˈedʒənsi] (n.)
   經紀公司，代理商

At the same time, she realized that the music industry in Kosovo was too small to satisfy her ambitions of a [4)]**career** in music. For this reason, she made a brave decision to return to London--alone.

與此同時，她意識到科索沃的音樂圈太小，無法滿足她追尋音樂生涯的野心。於是她做了一個大膽的決定，她要回倫敦，而且是隻身一人。

Back in the United Kingdom, Lipa completed her studies, then [5)]**enrolled** in the *****prestigious** Sylvia Young Theatre School, where she had previously taken singing classes. She began uploading her own songs and covers of famous artists to [6)]**websites** such as [LG)]**SoundCloud** and YouTube. At the same time, she joined a modeling [7)]**agency**, which helped her land a role in a commercial for *The X Factor*--a popular British *****reality TV** singing competition—in 2013. Playing **the girl next door**, she sang "Lost in Music," a [LG)]**disco** hit from the '70s, while hanging the washing in a garden.

回到英國後，黎波完成了學業，然後進入知名學府西爾維亞楊戲劇學校就讀，過去她曾在這裡上過歌唱課。她開始在 SoundCloud 和 YouTube 等網站上傳自己的歌和翻唱知名歌手的作品。同時她加入了一間模特兒經紀公司，該舉幫她獲得在《X 音素》──英國 2013 年推出的熱門真人歌唱選秀節目──廣告中演出一個角色。她飾演的鄰家女孩在院子裡一邊晾著衣服，一邊唱著七〇年代的迪斯可金曲〈沉溺音樂〉。

ADVANCED WORDS

*****naysayer** [ˈneˌseɚ] (n.)
反對者，唱反調者

*****superstardom** [ˈsupɚˌstɑrdəm] (n.)
超級巨星的地位

*****prestigious** [prɛsˈtɪdʒəs] (a.)
著名的，有名望的

*****reality TV** (n.)
真人秀，實境節目

Though hardly remembered, even by fans, the appearance put her in the spotlight. Shortly after, she was signed by a record label and released her first single, "New Love." Her early songs were more successful in [1]**mainland** Europe and Australia, and it wasn't till her debut album in 2017 that she made her U.K. [2]**breakthrough**. Her second album "Future *****Nostalgia**" topped the U.K. charts in 2020. The following year it rose to number three on the *Billboard* 200 chart in the U.S. Grammys and other awards followed.

儘管沒什麼人記得這支廣告，連粉絲都不記得，這次露臉卻讓她成為矚目焦點。不久她就被一間唱片公司簽下，發行了首張單曲〈新歡〉。她早期的歌曲在歐洲大陸和澳洲比較紅，在英國則是到 2017 年首張專輯發行才有所突破。2020 年發行的第二張專輯《流行先鋒》在英國排行榜奪冠，隔年專輯在美國拿下告示牌二百大專輯榜第三名，之後更獲得葛萊美獎與其他大獎的肯定。

[3]**Despite** her success --which includes a big screen [LG]**cameo** in *Barbie*--Lipa has admitted to suffering [4]**anxiety**, <u>brought on</u> by the stress of running her own social media accounts.

儘管事業發展成功，包含在電影《芭比》中客串演出，黎波坦承經營社群媒體的壓力導致她產生焦慮。

Handing control of the accounts to a team helped ease the pressure. The experience made her [5]**sympathetic** to mental health problems, and she has

---

VOCABULARY

1. **mainland** [ˈmenˌlænd] (a./n.)
   大陸（的），本土（的）
2. **breakthrough** [ˈbrekˌθru] (n.)
   突破性進展
3. **despite** [dɪˈspaɪt] (prep.) 雖然，儘管
4. **anxiety** [æŋˈzaɪəti] (n.) 焦慮，不安

5. **sympathetic** [ˌsɪmpəˈθetɪk] (a.)
   有同情心的，同情的
6. **vulnerable** [ˈvʌlnəəbl] (a.)
   易受傷的，脆弱的
7. **immigrant** [ˈɪmɪgrənt] (n.) 移民，僑民
8. **minister** [ˈmɪnɪstə] (n.) 部長，大臣

publicly supported ***LGBTQ** friends, observing that they seemed particularly
[6]**vulnerable** during the Covid-19 ***pandemic**. Lipa has also supported minority
groups. As the child of Kosovo Albanians, she has objected to the negative
images of [7]**immigrants** in general and Albanians in particular. When the British
foreign [8]**minister** spoke of "Albanian criminals," Lipa called such descriptions
"***small-minded**" and admitted the words upset her. "Of course it hurt," she said.

她將社群媒體帳號交給團隊經營，減輕一點壓力。這段經歷讓她對心理健康問題非常同情，
她看到 LGBTQ 族群的朋友在新冠疫情期間特別脆弱，對他們公開表示支持。黎波也力挺少
數族群。由於自己就是科索沃阿爾巴尼亞族的孩子，她反對移民被塑造的負面形象，尤其是
阿爾巴尼亞移民。當英國外長提到「阿爾巴尼亞罪犯」時，黎波表示這種描述是「心胸狹
隘」，並坦承這樣的言詞讓她聽了很難過。「當然很受傷，」她說。

She was one of a group of more than 4,000 singers and actors who signed an
[LG]**open letter** to U.S. President Joe Biden calling for an immediate ***ceasefire** in
Israel's war in [LG]**Gaza**.

黎波也參與了四千多名歌手和演員給美國總統拜登的連署公開信，呼籲以色列在加薩走廊的
戰爭立即停火。

ADVANCED WORDS

* **nostalgia** [nɑsˋtældʒə] (n.) 懷舊
* **LGBTQ** (n.) 多元性別
* **pandemic** [pænˋdɛmɪk] (n.)
  大流行病，疫情
* **small-minded** [ˋsmɔlˋmaɪndɪd] (a.)
  心胸狹窄的

* **ceasefire** [ˋsɪsˌfaɪr] (n.)
  （通常指兩軍間的）停火，休戰

While Lipa makes her voice heard, she admits that some people don't like
[1)]**entertainers** to offer opinions about the news. "They don't want you to be political," she says.

雖然黎波敢於發聲，她承認有些人就是不喜歡藝人對時事發表意見。「他們不希望你跟政治沾上邊，」她說。

For most fans, it's Lipa's singing voice that appeals. Her tone is described as "*****throaty** and mature." It is suited to EDM and is sometimes electronically [2)]**manipulated**, creating a *****haunting** echo. The U.K. No. 1 hit "New Rules" is one example. Other popular songs include "Don't Start Now" and "Levitating."

大多數粉絲都是被黎波的嗓音所吸引。她的聲調被形容為「低沉而成熟」，非常適合唱電子舞曲，有時透過電子後製創造縈繞回音效果。英國冠軍單曲〈愛情守則〉就是一例。另外像〈拒絕再玩〉、〈興致高昂〉都是夯曲。

In this way, Dua Lipa has turned her voice from a weakness into a weapon. After her early [3)]**rejection**, she must feel deep pride.

如此一來，杜娃黎波將她的聲音從劣勢轉為優勢。在經歷兒時被拒之後，她現在一定為自己獨樹一格的低沉嗓音感到自豪。

VOCABULARY

1. **entertainer** [ˌɛntəˈtenɚ] (n.)
   表演者，藝人
2. **manipulate** [məˈnɪpjəˌlet] (v.)
   操縱，操控
3. **rejection** [rɪˈdʒɛkʃən] (n.)
   拒絕，退回

ADVANCED WORDS

* ***throaty** [ˈθroti] (a.)
   （聲音）低沉的、沙啞的
* ***haunting** [ˈhɔntɪŋ] (a.) 令人難忘的

LANGUAGE GUIDE (LG)

lead vocalist 主唱

又可稱為 main vocalist 或是 lead singer，是在音樂團體中負責主要歌唱部份的成員，他們負責的部分旋律最為突出，主唱可能被視為樂團的團長或代言人。

rock 搖滾樂

起源於四〇年代末期英國和美國，五〇年代開始大為風行，為 rock and roll 的簡稱。現在的搖滾樂泛指所有具備搖滾風格的樂曲。

Kosovo 科索沃 / Albanian 阿爾巴尼亞語

位於歐洲巴爾幹半島的國家，在 1990 年代末期透過戰爭脫離塞爾維亞並宣布獨立，但塞爾維亞至今仍不承認其獨立，故時有衝突。Kosovar 為科索沃人，或科索沃相關事物，阿爾巴尼亞語 (Albanian) 為科索沃的官方語言之一。

Pink 紅粉佳人

美國歌手與詞曲作家，音樂類型為流行與流行搖滾，出道時以搶眼的粉紅短髮、演唱功力與辛辣敢言的形象受到矚目。曾獲葛萊美「最佳搖滾女歌手」、全英音樂獎「最佳國際女藝人」等多項大獎。

SoundCloud

線上音樂串流平臺，總部位於德國柏林，供音樂人上傳音樂，使用者關注和轉發，平臺於 2007 年創立，已發展為最大的音樂串流媒體服務商之一。

disco 迪斯可音樂

是一種舞曲音樂，特點是強勁的節拍和穩定的節奏，常伴隨合成器和電子鼓。來自 1970 年美國紐約。以其歡快的節奏、朗朗上口的旋律和重複的歌詞而聞名。

cameo 客串演出

在一部電影的某些場景中短暫出現的演員稱之為 cameo 或 cameo role。用法是 Sb. makes / has a cameo in... 或是 Sb. makes / has a cameo appearance in...。這個字也同時可以當動詞用。

open letter 公開信

公開信是在報紙或雜誌上發表的一封信。它是針對特定的個人或團體，但內容公開發表，讓大眾都能知道。通常是為了抗議或對某件事發表意見。

Gaza 加薩走廊

位於埃及和以色列中間，為 Gaza Strip（加薩走廊）的簡稱。由於信仰與歷史因素，為以色列和巴勒斯坦極力爭取的土地，衝突不斷。

PHRASES

the apple doesn't fall far from the tree 有其父（母）必有其子（女）

此片語字面上的意思為「蘋果落地後，離樹不遠」，引申為孩子和父母的個性與資質相似，也就是「有其父（母）必有其子（女）」。

A Felix is really good at tennis, just like his father.
費利克斯在網球方面真的很厲害，就像他父親一樣。

B Well, **the apple doesn't fall far from the tree**.
嗯，果然有其父必有其子。

follow suit 仿效，跟風

suit 的意思為「同花色的一組紙牌」，follow suit 就是跟著別人的花色出牌，也可引伸為「跟風」，和別人一起，一窩蜂做一樣的事，就可用 follow suit。

A I notice this new product is available in lots of supermarkets now.
我注意到這個新產品現在在很多超市都有販售。

B Yup. After the first store started selling it, the others quickly **followed suit**.
對啊，第一家店開始賣後，其他店很快就開始仿效。

have egg on one's face （某人）丟臉，出醜

此片語其中一個可能的出處為 19 世紀初，在劇場表演較差的演員可能會被丟雞蛋，而後當某人做了愚蠢的事，就可以用 have egg on one's face 來形容。

A My friend said I would fail this exam!
我朋友說我這次考試會不及格！

B I guess he **had egg on his face** when you got such a high grade.
我猜他在你得了這麼高分時一定感到很尷尬。

the girl next door 鄰家女孩

由於電影中的 the girl next door 常常住在主角的隔壁，一開始和主角間是純友誼，後來往往和主角交往。這個片語通常指看起來「自然、善良、好相處」的女子。

◎ The actress played **the girl next door** early in her career, before starring in several action movies.
這位女演員在主演幾部動作片之前，在早期職業生涯中都飾演鄰家女孩。

◎ Despite her image as **the girl next door**, Helen liked to party.
儘管她被塑造成鄰家女孩的形象，海倫喜歡狂歡。

bring sth. on 引起，造成

此片語表示「讓某件不愉快的事發生在某人身上」，這些事件可以是災難 (disaster)、疾病 (illness)、難題 (dilemma)。

A What **brought on** your sudden illness?
你突然生病是怎麼回事？

B I think it may have been something I ate.
我想可能是我吃了什麼不對勁的東西。

QUOTES

關於自己的偶像

"I love Pink and Nelly Furtado--the honesty and truth in their lyrics. I also love Kendrick Lamar and Chance the Rapper."

我喜歡粉紅佳人和妮莉費塔朵，喜歡他們歌詞裡的誠實和真實。我也喜歡肯卓克拉瑪和饒舌錢斯。

表演如何融入生活

"My parents never pushed me towards music. I feel like, growing up in a musical household and always being surrounded by it, I was always kind of a performer child. I remember my parents would have guests over, and they would bring their kids, and I would make sure that we were ready to put a show on."

我父母從沒刻意要我走音樂的路。我覺得，在一個音樂家庭長大，生活裡都是音樂，向來就是個愛表演的小孩。我記得爸媽會邀請客人來，他們都會帶小孩，我就確保大家來場精彩演出。

變得更愛自己

"I'm learning to accept myself. I'm still in the process of learning to love who I am. And it's been really refreshing and really nice to be able to do that and be OK. I think my fans have brought that out in me."

我正在學習接納自己。我仍處於學習愛自己的過程。能夠愛自己而且感到自在，真的很舒暢很美好。我覺得是粉絲讓我有所改變。

關於性別歧視

"For a female artist, it takes a lot more to be taken seriously if you're not sat down at a piano or with a guitar, you know?"

你知道嗎？對一個女歌手而言，假如妳不是坐在鋼琴前或背把吉他，妳就需要付出更多努力才會被認真看待。

關於時尚

"I like how powerful fashion makes me feel. I live for that grungy-prissy juxtaposition that Kate Moss, Naomi Campbell, and Drew Barrymore wore in the '90s."

我喜歡時尚讓我感覺充滿力量。我超愛凱特摩絲、娜歐蜜坎貝兒和茱兒芭莉摩他們九〇年代那種頹廢又拘謹的混搭。

對自己的期許

"Every time you achieve something, you want to go after what's next. I'd like to see my own shows grow and someday be a headliner, fill up stadiums."

每當你達成一項成就，你就想追求下一個目標。我希望看到自己的表演不斷成長，有朝一日當主打藝人，體育館場場爆滿。

關於成功

"Success, to me, is just doing things that I'm really proud of."

對我而言，成功就是做我真正引以為豪的事。

關於心態

"I always told myself never to have a plan B. I feel like that's also one of the reasons I'm doing what I'm doing now, because I just never really rested until I got here."

我總是告訴自己不要留退路。我覺得我現在能做這些事情，這是其中一個原因，我未曾真正停歇才有今天的成就。

Drake
德瑞克
從迪格拉西到制霸樂壇

© Shutterstock.com

德瑞克是第一位打進美國與國際嘻哈市場的非美籍饒舌歌手,最早以電視影集起家的他,在嘻哈音樂中確立自身地位。成名致富後,仍致力維護隱私,在音樂方面也掌握串流密碼,並且持續和新人合作,也難怪他能維持串流之王的地位。

From Degrassi to Dominance

In the world of rap and R&B, few names shine as brightly as Drake's. Born in Toronto to an African-American father from Memphis, Tennessee and a ***Jewish** Canadian mother, Aubrey Drake Graham grew up with music in his blood. His father was a drummer who once worked with rock 1)**legend** LG)**Jerry Lee Lewis**, and his uncle played 2)**bass** for Sly and the Family Stone.

在饒舌和節奏藍調的世界裡，很少有名字像德瑞克這般耀眼。德瑞克出生於多倫多，父親是來自田納西州曼菲斯的非裔美國人，母親則是猶太裔加拿大人。奧布里德瑞克葛拉罕從小就流著音樂的血液，他的父親是一名鼓手，曾和搖滾傳奇傑瑞李路易斯一同表演，而他的叔伯則是史萊和史東家族合唱團的貝斯手。

VOCABULARY

1. legend [ˈlɛdʒənd] (n.)
傳說，傳奇人物
2. bass [bes] (n.)
貝斯吉他，低音提琴

ADVANCED WORDS

* **Jewish** [ˈdʒuɪʃ] (a.)
猶太人的，猶太教的

As a black kid who went to Jewish day school, Drake was [1])**bullied** due to his ethnic and religious identity. Perhaps because of this, he became the class clown, a role that led to his first break at 15. "I used to always <u>crack jokes</u> in class," says Drake. "And this kid in my class was like, "Yo, my dad is an [2])**agent**. You should go talk to him because you're good, and you make people laugh."" After a successful audition, the agent helped Drake land the role of Jimmy Brooks—a basketball star who becomes [3])**disabled** after being shot by a classmate—on the popular Canadian teen drama [LG)]*Degrassi: The Next Generation*.

身為黑人小孩，念的卻是猶太日校，種族和宗教身分導致德瑞克遭受霸凌。也許是因為這個原因，他成了班上的活寶，沒想到這成為他十五歲人生第一次走紅的契機。「我以前在班上一直開玩笑，」德瑞克說，「班上有個小孩就說：『喲，我老爹是經紀人，你很厲害又會逗人笑，你該去跟他談談。』」通過試鏡之後，這位經紀人幫他爭取到加拿大熱門青少年影集《德格拉西：下一代》中的吉米布魯克斯一角。吉米是一位籃球明星，因遭同學槍擊導致身殘。

But how did Drake's musical *__inclinations__ develop? His parents got [4])**divorced** when he was still a child, and his father moved back to Memphis. Drake would visit him each summer, and on the long car ride south listening to his dad's favorite music—Al Green, The Spinners, Marvin Gaye—he developed an [5])**appreciation** for the melody and emotion of classic R&B and [LG)]**soul music**. His dad was later *__incarcerated__ on drug [6])**charges**, and he shared his phone time with his *__cellmate__, who liked to rap for the young Drake. Before long, he was

VOCABULARY

1. **bully** [ˋbʊli] (v.) 欺凌
2. **agent** [ˋedʒənt] (n.) 經紀人
3. **disabled** [dɪsˋebəld] (a.) 殘疾的
4. **divorce** [dɪˋvors] (v.) 離婚
5. **appreciation** [əˌpriʃiˋeʃən] (n.) 欣賞
6. **charge** [tʃɑrdʒ] (n.) 指控，控告

7. **lyric** [ˋlɪrɪk] (n.)
   歌詞（固定用複數 **lyrics**）

filling notebooks with his own rap ⁷⁾**lyrics**.

德瑞克又是怎麼發展出他的音樂傾向的？他父母在他小時候離異，之後父親搬回曼菲斯居住。每年夏天德瑞克都會去拜訪父親，在搭車前往南方的長途旅行中，德瑞克會聽著父親最愛的音樂，像是阿爾格林、編織者合唱團、馬文蓋，於是開始懂得欣賞經典節奏藍調和靈魂樂中的旋律和情感。後來父親被控涉毒入獄，和獄友分享父子的通話時間，獄友很愛唱饒舌給年輕的德瑞克聽。沒過多久，德瑞克就在筆記本上寫滿自己創作的饒舌歌詞了。

After several seasons on *Degrassi*, Drake realized that music was his true passion, and started staying up half the night writing and recording songs. When the studio complained about him showing up late on set, he **talked the security guards into** letting him sleep in his dressing room. Drake released his first ^{LG)}**mixtape**, *Room for Improvement*, in 2006, but it only sold 6,000 copies. His next mixtape, 2007's *Comeback Season*, didn't fare much better. But it did **catch the ear of** New Orleans rapper ^{LG)}**Lil Wayne**, who was so impressed that he invited Drake to fly down to Houston and join him on his *Tha Carter III* tour.

演出幾季的《德格拉西》後，德瑞克明白音樂才是他真正的愛好，開始熬夜創作和錄製歌曲。攝影棚抱怨他老是遲到，他就說服警衛讓他睡在自己的更衣室。2006 年他發行了個人第一張混音帶《改善空間》，但只賣了六千張。2007 年推出的下一張混音帶《卷土重來》也好不到哪裡去，不過倒是吸引了紐奧良饒舌歌手小韋恩的注意，他實在太喜歡德瑞克的音樂，便邀德瑞克飛來休士頓加入他的《卡特先生 III》世界巡演。

ADVANCED WORDS

* **inclination** [ɪnklə`neʃən] (n.)
  傾向，愛好
* **incarcerate** [ɪn`kɑrsə͵ret] (v.)
  監禁，禁閉
* **cellmate** [`sɛl͵met] (n.) 同室囚犯

While touring with Lil Wayne gained Drake valuable [1]**exposure**, it didn't do much for his bank account. "The money from that show was very small," says Drake, who left *Degrassi* in 2008. "And it was *****dwindling**." But things were about to change. In 2009, with Lil Wayne as his mentor, he finally achieved commercial success with his third mixtape, *So Far Gone*, which peaked at No. 5 on the *Billboard* 200 and *****spawned** two hit singles, "Successful" and "Best I Ever Had"—his first top ten hit.

和小韋恩一同巡演讓德瑞克得到寶貴的曝光度，卻對他的戶頭沒什麼幫助。「那巡演帶來的收入很少，」2008 年離開《德格拉西》的德瑞克說，「而且還不斷減少。」但是情況就要有所不同了。2009 年在小韋恩的指導下，德瑞克推出了第三張混音帶《一路走來》，終於取得了商業上的成功，登上告示牌二百大專輯榜的第五名，還催生了兩首熱門單曲〈成功〉和〈我曾擁有的最美好〉，後者是他第一支打進排行前十的單曲。

After a big bidding war, Drake signed with Lil Wayne's Young Money Records and started working on his debut album. Released to much [2]**anticipation** in 2010, *Thank Me Later* debuted at No. 1 on the *Billboard* 200, introducing larger audiences to Drake's [3]**unique** mix of rap and R&B. With help from Lil Wayne, Kanye West and Jay-Z, the album produced hits like "Over" and "Find Your Love," which were both [4]**nominated** for Grammys.

經過一番激烈的出價爭奪戰，德瑞克最終與小韋恩所創的年輕金錢唱片公司簽約，開始籌備他的第一張專輯。2010 年，《不急著道謝》專輯於萬眾期待之下發行，一推出便空降告示牌二百大專輯榜的冠軍，讓更多聽眾認識他融合饒舌與節奏藍調的獨特曲風。在小韋恩、肯

VOCABULARY

1. exposure [ɪk`spoʒə] (n.) 曝光，暴露

2. anticipation [æn͵tɪsə`peʃən] (n.) 期望，盼望

3. unique [ju`nik] (a.) 獨特的，獨一無二的

4. nominate [`nɑmə͵net] (v.) 提名

5. refine [rɪ`faɪn] (v.) 提煉，精煉

6. highlight [`haɪ͵laɪt] (n.) 最精采、有趣的部分

7. reflect [rɪ`flɛkt] (v.) 反射，反映

8. awkwardly [`ɔkwədli] (adv.) 尷尬地，笨拙地

伊威斯特和傑斯的助陣之下，專輯誕生出〈結束〉、〈得到你的愛〉等熱門歌曲，兩支單曲都入圍了葛萊美獎。

Drake continued to [5]**refine** his blend of singing and rapping on his next two albums, 2011's *Take Care*, which won a Grammy for Best Rap Album, and 2013's *Nothing Was the Same*, which debuted on top of the *Billboard* 200. [6]**Highlights** from the albums include "Take Care," a *****duet** with Rihanna that [7]**reflected** their complex real-life relationship; and "Started from the Bottom," a *****catchy** hit single about his rise to fame.

在接下來的兩張專輯中，德瑞克持續精進他的歌唱饒舌融合曲風。2011 年發行的《呵護》獲得葛萊美獎最佳饒舌專輯，2013 年的《物換星移》則空降告示牌二百大專輯榜首。兩張專輯的重點單曲包括了與蕾哈娜合唱的〈呵護〉，這首歌反映了兩人真實生活中的複雜關係，而〈從頭做起〉則描述他的成名之路，是一首琅琅上口的熱門單曲。

But it was Drake's fourth album, 2016's *Views*, that turned him into a global star. Influenced by Caribbean and African music, the album delivered the global hit singles "One Dance" and "Hotline Bling." "One Dance," featuring Nigerian singer Wizkid and a [LG]**dancehall** beat, reached No. 1 in 15 countries. "Hotline Bling," a **booty call** song set to a cha-cha rhythm, won Grammys for Best Rap Song and Best Rap/Sung Performance. And the video, which features Drake dancing [8]**awkwardly**, turned him into a cultural phenomenon, inspiring countless *****memes**.

ADVANCED WORDS

*****dwindle** [ˈdwɪndəl] (v.) 漸漸減少
*****spawn** [spɔn] (v.)（使）產生
*****duet** [duˋɛt] (n.) 二重唱
*****catchy** [ˈkætʃi] (a.) 動聽好記的
*****meme** [mim] (n.)
　梗圖（指「網路爆紅的搞笑圖片」）

然而一直要到第四張專輯，2016 年的《傲視》才讓他成為國際巨星。專輯受到加勒比和非洲音樂的影響，誕生出〈最後一舞〉和〈熱線響起〉兩支全球暢銷單曲。〈最後一舞〉邀來奈及利亞歌手 Wizkid 獻聲，採用一種舞廳雷鬼的拍子，登上十五個國家的排行榜第一。〈熱線響起〉則是一首設定為恰恰節奏的約炮歌，奪得最佳饒舌歌曲和最佳饒舌／演唱表演兩座葛萊美獎。德瑞克在音樂錄影帶中的尷尬舞步被做成各種梗圖，變成一種文化潮流。

Since [1]**attaining** superstar [2]**status**, Drake has continued to **crank out** No. 1 hits, like "God's Plan" and "In My Feelings" from 2018's double album *Scorpion*, and "Way 2 Sexy" from 2021's *Certified Lover Boy*, which set a record for the most top ten singles from one album (9). And somehow, Drake has still managed to find time for other [3]**endeavors**. He's created his own record label, [LG]**OVO Sound**, to provide opportunities for Canadian rap and R&B artists, as well as a fashion label, production company, and even a *****fragrance** house. Drake also serves as global ambassador for the [LG]**Toronto Raptors**, which may explain why he calls his $100 million mansion, which can be seen in his "Toosie Slide" video, "The [4]**Embassy**."

自從德瑞克躋身超級巨星之列，就不斷創造出多首冠軍單曲，像是 2018 年的雙碟裝專輯《蠍王》中的〈上帝旨意〉和〈感觸良多〉，還有 2021 年專輯《認證情聖》中的〈性感過頭〉。《認證情聖》還創下一張專輯擁有最多支排名前十單曲（九支）的紀錄。而且德瑞克還能找出時間進行其他嘗試。他創立了自己的唱片公司 OVO Sound，讓加拿大的饒舌和節奏藍調歌手能有發展的機會，還擁有個人的時尚品牌、製作公司和香水品牌。德瑞克也擔任多倫多暴龍的全球形象大使，這也許可以解釋為什麼他要把他價值一億美元的豪宅命名為「大使館」了。透過〈Toosie 滑步〉這首歌的音樂錄影帶，觀眾得以一窺這座豪宅面貌。

VOCABULARY

1. **attain** [əˋten] (v.) 獲得，達到
2. **status** [ˋstætəs] (n.) 地位，身分
3. **endeavor** [ɪnˋdɛvə] (n.)
   努力，嘗試
4. **embassy** [ˋɛmbəsi] (n.)
   大使館

ADVANCED WORDS

***fragrance** [ˋfregrəns] (n.)
香水，香味

LANGUAGE GUIDE (LG)

Jerry Lee Lewis 傑瑞李路易斯

美國唱作歌手、音樂人，音樂類型為搖滾、鄉村等，被暱稱為 The Killer（殺手），獲頒「葛萊美終身成就獎」，並被《滾石雜誌》列為「有史以來一百個最偉大藝術家」之一。

Degrassi: The Next Generation 德格拉西：下一代

加拿大青少年電視影集，於 2001 年 10 月在 CTV 首播，並於 2015 年 8 月在 MTV Canada 結束。主要講述青春期學生所面臨的問題與挑戰。在最初播映的幾年間，經常為加拿大收視率最高的國產電視劇。

soul music 靈魂樂

起源於 1950 年代的美國，在流行樂中加入節奏藍調和福音音樂的要素。緊扣節奏、拍掌、即興形體動作，是其重要特色。

mixtape 混音帶

為自製的音樂合輯，裡面通常是一些已發表的音樂創作加上自己的混音串連起來的專輯，樂者藉由 mixtape 來表達自己對音樂的想法。會使用前人的音樂片段，即興創作後錄下來後再製，所以裡面會有很多有版權的音樂，算是未經授權的二次創作。

Lil Wayne 小韋恩

美國饒舌歌手與唱片公司執行長，音樂類型為嘻哈、節奏藍調，已獲 5 次葛萊美獎、2 次 MTV 音樂錄影帶大獎。在 2012 年 9 月 27 日，韋恩超越貓王成為登上告示牌百大熱門榜次數最多的男藝人（共 109 首單曲登榜）。

dancehall 舞廳雷鬼

是牙買加流行音樂的一種流派，起源於 20 世紀 70 年代末牙買加，是雷鬼音樂的一種。

OVO Sound

加拿大獨立唱片公司，2012 年於加拿大創立，創辦人為饒舌歌手 Drake、製作人 40 和經理 Oliver El-Khatib，主要音樂類型為嘻哈、陷阱、節奏藍調。

Toronto Raptors 多倫多暴龍隊

位於多倫多的加拿大職業籃球隊，為 NBA 東區聯盟唯一一支加拿大球隊。從 1995 年創立。2019 年季後賽，暴龍隊贏得了他們的第一個東部冠軍頭銜，首次闖入 NBA 總決賽，並贏得了他們的第一個 NBA 總冠軍。

PHRASES

crack a joke 開玩笑，說俏皮話

crack 有「大聲說、發音、講述」的意思，因此 crack a joke 就是「講笑話、說俏皮話」的意思。

A Didn't you say Alex was the class clown?
　 你不是說亞歷克斯是班上的活寶嗎？

B Yeah. He's always **cracking jokes** in class.
　 是啊。他總是在課堂上說笑話。

talk (sb.) into 說服

說服某人做（某事）　說服別人去做一件事，除了用 persuade [pəˋswed] 這個動詞外，還有個更簡單的 talk sb. into... 後接動詞加 ing；若是要「說服某人不做（某事）」則是用 talk sb. out of... 即可。

A He said no to our request.
　 他拒絕我們的要求。

B You'll just have to **talk him into** it.
　 你得說服他啊。

catch the ear of 引起某人注意

表示「用聲音吸引某人注意、引起某人的興趣（特別是聽覺上有吸引力）」，後面會加某人或某物，也可以用 catch one's ear 來表達。

◎ The singer's YouTube video **caught the ear of** several record labels.
　 這位歌手的 YouTube 影片引起了幾家唱片公司的注意。

◎ A strange sound in the woods **caught the** hiker's **ear**.
　 森林裡一陣奇怪的聲音引起了登山客的注意。

booty call 約炮，炮友

booty 有「屁股」的意思，同時也是「性行為」的委婉說法。booty call 的意思為「約炮」和「炮友」。

◎ Jennifer Lopez says that Drake was just a **booty call**.
　珍妮佛羅培茲說德雷克只是她的炮友而已。

◎ If he's texting you after midnight, it's obviously a **booty call**.
　如果他在午夜後發簡訊給你，顯然是在約炮。

crank out 大量生產

通常指人或公司，大量且快速的生產某產品，但可能因此而非原創或品質不佳。

◎ The author manages to **crank out** a new novel every year.
　這位作者每年能寫出一部新小說。

◎ Reporters at the paper are required to **crank out** at least an article a day.
　報社的記者們被要求至少每天寫一篇文章。

QUOTES

談論自己的個性

"I'm not confrontational, but if someone challenges, I'm not going to back down."

我不會咄咄逼人，但如果有人挑釁，我是不會退縮的。

"I've never been reckless - it's always calculated. I'm mischievous, but I'm calculated."

我從不衝動行事，都是深思熟慮過的。我很調皮，但也是深思熟慮的。

談論如何致富

"Rappers aren't the really rich ones. We all have nice houses with studios and cars, but you need a piece of someone's business to be super wealthy."

饒舌歌手不是真正的有錢人。我們都住豪宅，有工作室有車子，但你必須參與其他事業才能變超級富豪。

談論成功的定義

"I don't measure my success anymore by the Grammys. I can't because I'll just end up crushed."

我已經不再用葛萊美獎來衡量我的成功。我不行，因為那只會讓我很沮喪。

談論寫歌

"I push myself in a lot of aspects when I write a song. I write a piece and where most people would stop and say, 'Oh, that's the hook right there,' I'll move that to the first four bars of the verse and do a new hook."

寫歌時我會多方鞭策自己。每當寫好一段，如果大部分的人都停下來說：「喔，這段很有記憶點。」我就會把它挪到主歌的前四節，然後再寫一段記憶點。

對音樂的態度

"I feel that when you care about your music, taking risks is something you should do to keep things exciting."

我覺得當你在乎你的音樂，冒險就是你該做的事，才能讓音樂保持新鮮。

對舞台表演的想法

"When I'm writing, I'm thinking about how the songs are going to play live. Fifty bars of rap don't translate onstage. No matter how potent the music, you lose the crowd. They want a hook; they want to sing your stuff back to you."

我在寫歌的時候，會設想現場表演的樣子。五十節的饒舌在舞臺上是行不通的。無論你的音樂有多強大，觀眾都無法參與。他們要的是記憶點，他們想要跟你一起唱。

自己音樂的獨特性

"There were people who incorporated melody before me, but I would deem myself the first person to successfully rap and sing."

在我之前已經有人把旋律加進來，但我認為成功融合饒舌和歌唱的，我是第一人。

關於音樂

"I would say that I'm more moved by melody, even though I love to rap."

雖然我愛唱饒舌，我得說旋律更能感動我。

Ed Sheeran
紅髮艾德
從平凡的小鎮男孩到全球流行巨星

© FashionStock.com / Shutterstock.com

艾德在 1991 年出生於英國北部西約克郡,為英國創作歌手、音樂製作人,曲風為流行與民謠歌手,在全球共取得了 2600 萬專輯和 1 億單曲銷量,是世界暢銷音樂藝人之一,以樸實耐聽的歌曲打動了全球歌迷的心。

From Humble Beginnings to Global Pop Star

Unless you've been <u>living under a rock</u>, you've heard of Ed Sheeran. And if you have ears, you've heard his music. But do you know the story of how he went from small town boy to global pop *icon? Born on February 17, 1991 in Halifax, West Yorkshire into an [1]artistic family, Edward Christopher Sheeran showed an early *penchant for music. After moving to the even smaller town of Framlingham, Suffolk—population 3,114—young Ed began singing in the church choir at the age of four.

除非你與世隔絕，否則你一定聽過紅髮艾德。有耳朵你就一定聽過他的歌。但你知道他是如何從一個小鎮男孩成為全球流行偶像的嗎？ 1991 年 2 月 17 日，艾德華克里斯多夫希蘭出生於西約克郡哈利法克斯的一個藝術世家，小小年紀就展現對音樂的愛好。後來他們搬到一個更小的城鎮，人口只有 3,114 人、薩福克郡的弗拉姆林厄姆，年僅四歲的小艾德便加入了教會的唱詩班。

VOCABULARY

1. **artistic** [ɑrˋtɪstɪk] (a.)
   藝術的，有藝術天分的

ADVANCED WORDS

* **icon** [ˋaɪkɑn] (n.) 偶像，代表性人物
* **penchant** [ˋpɛntʃənt] (n.) 偏好，傾向

When Ed—an ¹⁾**awkward** boy with red hair, big glasses and a ²⁾**stutter**—was bullied at school, it was music that saved him. Rap, to be specific. His uncle bought him an ᴸᴳ⁾**Eminem** CD when he was nine, and within a year his stutter was cured. "I learned every word of it by the time I was 10," says Sheeran, "and it helped me get rid of the stutter." Recognizing their son's gift, his parents bought him his first guitar. By the age of 11, Sheeran was ³⁾**composing** his own songs, ⁴⁾**inspired** by his musical heroes, ᴸᴳ⁾**Bob Dylan**, ᴸᴳ⁾**Elton John** and ᴸᴳ⁾**Eric Clapton**.

當艾德——一頭紅髮又四眼田雞，說話結結巴巴、看起來放不開的男孩—在學校被同學欺負時，是音樂給了他救贖。說得確切一點是饒舌音樂。艾德九歲的時候，叔叔買了一張阿姆的 CD 唱片給他，不到一年他的口吃竟然好了。「我十歲就把整張專輯背得滾瓜爛熟，」希蘭說，「我的口吃就這樣治好了。」父母看出了兒子的天賦，買了他人生中的第一把吉他給他。在其音樂偶像巴布狄倫、艾爾頓強和艾瑞克克萊普頓的啟發之下，希蘭十一歲就開始寫歌。

Confident in his abilities, Sheeran ⁵⁾**dropped out** of high school at the age of 16 and moved to London. He played hundreds of shows at small pubs, and even *****busked** on the streets, to <u>make ends meet</u>. When he couldn't afford a place to stay, he slept on friends' couches, and sometimes subway trains. But Sheeran's love of music kept him going, and with his natural talent and charm, he began drawing larger crowds. He also posted videos on YouTube, where his songs—which combine pop, ᴸᴳ⁾**folk** and ᴸᴳ⁾**soft rock**—and of course his ⁶⁾**ginger *mop**,

---

VOCABULARY

1. awkward [ˋɔkwəd] (a.)
尷尬的，笨拙的

2. stutter [ˋstʌtə] (n.)
口吃，說話結結巴巴

3. compose [kəmˋpoz] (v.)
作曲，創作（音樂、詩）

4. inspire [ɪnˋspaɪr] (v.)
賦予……靈感，激勵

5. drop out [drɑp aʊt] (phr.) 輟學

6. ginger [ˋdʒɪndʒə] (a.) 薑黃色的

attracted lots of attention.

希蘭對自己的能力充滿信心，十六歲自高中輟學來到倫敦闖蕩。他靠著在小酒吧的數百場演出，甚至在街頭賣藝以維持生計。付不起房租的時候，他就到朋友家睡沙發，有時還夜宿地鐵站。然而對音樂的熱愛讓希蘭堅持了下去，憑藉著音樂天賦與個人魅力，他開始吸引更大的聽眾。他也在 YouTube 上分享影片，曲風結合流行、民謠和抒情搖滾，而他的歌曲，當然還有那一頭紅髮，獲得了大量關注。

But it wasn't until a trip to L.A. in 2010 that Sheeran got his **big break**. While going around to radio stations with ***demos** of his songs, he ran into ^{LG)}**Jamie Foxx**—yes, *that* Jamie Foxx. Foxx was so impressed with his music that he asked Sheeran to perform on his radio show, and even let him stay at his mansion and use his music studio. This exposure led to a record deal with Asylum Records, which Elton John, also a fan, helped arrange.

但直到 2010 年的洛杉磯行，希蘭才獲得職業生涯的突破。當時他帶著自己的試聽帶到處跑電臺，遇上了傑米福克斯——對，就是「那個」傑米福克斯。福克斯對他的音樂十分激賞，邀他來上自己的廣播節目，還讓他住自己的豪宅、用自己的音樂工作室。這次的曝光加上身為歌迷的艾爾頓強居中安排，促成了他與庇護所唱片公司簽約。

ADVANCED WORDS

★**busk** [bʌsk] (v.) 街頭表演，街頭賣藝
★**mop** [mɑp] (n.)
　濃密、不整齊的頭髮，原意為「拖把」
★**demo** [ˋdɛmo] (n.) 試聽帶，樣本唱片

Sheeran's debut album, + (pronounced "plus"), was released in 2011. The lead single, "The A Team," a sad, tender tale about a female drug [1]**addict** who lives on the streets, introduced him as an artist who knew how to tell stories. The song peaked at No. 3 in the U.K, and the album at No. 1. Sheeran was now huge in his home country, but it took Taylor Swift to make him popular <u>across the pond</u>.

2011 年希蘭發表首張專輯《+》（讀作 plus，加法），首發單曲〈A 咖一族〉講述一名毒品成癮女子流落街頭的故事，悲傷而令人動容，讓他成為一個會說故事的歌手。這首歌在英國拿下排行榜第三名，專輯則衝上排行榜冠軍。此時希蘭在自己國家已經非常火紅，不過在美國，卻是靠著泰勒絲才紅了起來。

After hearing Sheeran's music, Swift invited him to sing a duet with her on "Everything Has Changed" for her 2012 album *Red*, and then open for her on the Red Tour the following year. What better way to get famous than share the stage with Taylor Swift at [2]**arenas** all across the U.S.? He was even invited to perform "The A Team" with Elton John at the 2013 Grammy Awards!

泰勒絲聽了希蘭的音樂便邀他合唱〈都變了〉，收錄在 2012 年的專輯《紅色》，隔年更邀他在紅色巡演中擔任開場嘉賓。還有什麼比跟著泰勒絲跑遍全美體育館還同臺演出更好的成名方式？他甚至受邀在 2013 年的葛萊美頒獎典禮上與艾爾頓強一同演唱〈A 咖一族〉呢！

But it was Sheeran's [3]**sophomore** album, x ("multiply"), that brought him global fame. Released in 2014, the album topped the charts in both the U.K. and the

---

VOCABULARY

1. **addict** [ˈædɪkt] (n.) 成癮者
2. **arena** [əˈrinə] (n.) 體育場，表演場地
3. **sophomore** [ˈsɑfˌmor]
   二年級的，第二章（專輯等）
4. **exhausted** [ɪgˈzɔstəd] (a.) 筋疲力竭的
5. **inspiration** [ˌɪnspəˈreʃən] (n.) 靈感

6. **gross** [gros] (v.)
   獲得……總收入（或毛利）

U.S., reaching No. 1 in 15 countries. Sheeran's *multitude of fans were dancing in the clubs to R&B hit "Sing" (produced by Pharrell), and getting married to the romantic *ballad "Thinking Out Loud," which won two Grammys, including Song of the Year.

不過一直到希蘭的第二張專輯《x》（讀作 multiply，乘法）推出後，他才紅遍全球。2014 年發行的這張專輯不僅在英美霸榜，同時在十五個國家都登上第一。希蘭的眾多粉絲或在夜店裡隨著他的節奏藍調名曲〈歡唱〉（由菲董製作）跳舞，或在婚禮上播放他的浪漫情歌〈自言自語〉，而這首歌也一舉拿下包括年度歌曲在內的兩項葛萊美獎。

At this point, 4)exhausted from performing, touring, and always being in the public eye, Sheeren decided to take a year-long *hiatus from music and social media. He traveled the world, spent time with friends and family, and sought 5)inspiration for his next album. He must have found it, because 2017's ÷ ("divide") was the best-selling album in the world that year! And on the strength of songs like "Shape of You"—the hit single originally written for Rihanna—Sheeran's Divide Tour was the highest 6)grossing in history.

就在此時，不停地演出、巡迴和總是大眾關注焦點讓希蘭覺得好累，決定暫別音樂和社群媒體休息一年。他環遊世界，和家人朋友相聚，並為下一張專輯尋找靈感。他肯定是找到了，因為 2017 年的《÷》（讀作 divide，除法）榮登該年全球最暢銷專輯！挾著暢銷單曲〈你的樣子〉（原本是寫給蕾哈娜唱的）等強力曲目的氣勢，希蘭的除法巡演成為史上最賺錢的巡迴演出。

ADVANCED WORDS

* **multitude** [ˋmʌltəˌtud] (n.)
  眾多（人事物）
* **ballad** [ˋbæləd] (n.) 情歌，慢歌
* **hiatus** [haɪˋetəs] (n.) 暫停，休息

But has Sheeran been as lucky in love as in his career? His relationship with Scottish singer Nina Nesbitt didn't last long, and he [1]**broke up** with TV [2]**chef** Jamie Oliver's assistant Athina Andrelos because she got jealous of his female fans. But <u>the third time was the charm</u>. Sheeran invited childhood sweetheart Cherry Seaborn to a Taylor Swift party in 2015, and they were soon dating. He married Seaborn in secret three years later, but his feelings for her are no secret. In "Perfect," he sings, "I found a lover, to carry more than just my secrets / To carry love, to carry children of our own." Let's hope his wife and two daughters, Jupiter and Lyra, will inspire new hits for years to come!

希蘭的感情世界是否和演唱事業一樣幸運呢？他和蘇格蘭歌手妮娜奈斯比特有過一段短命戀情，和傑米奧利佛的助理雅典娜安卓洛斯最後也以分手收場，因為她老是吃女粉絲的醋。不過第三次一定會成功。2015 年的時候，希蘭邀請他的青梅竹馬雪莉席邦來參加泰勒絲的派對，沒多久就開始交往。三年後兩人祕密結婚，他對她的情感則是毫不隱藏。他在〈完美無瑕〉一曲當中唱著：「我找到一個愛人，她守著我的祕密，對我付出真愛，孕育我倆的孩子。」讓我們期待在未來幾年，他的妻子和兩個女兒茉比特和萊拉能激發他寫出更多暢銷單曲！

VOCABULARY

1. break up [brek ˋʌp] (phr.)
   分手，（婚姻）破裂
2. chef [ʃɛf] (n.) 主廚

LANGUAGE GUIDE (LG)

Eminem 阿姆

1972 年出生，美國饒舌歌手、詞曲作家、唱片製作人，從小生活在黑人社區的阿姆，為饒舌界公認的第一快嘴，身為白人的他，卻在黑人當道的嘻哈圈闖出一片天，為史上最偉大的饒舌歌手之一。

Bob Dylan 巴布狄倫

出生於 1941 年，美國創作歌手與詞曲作家，又有民謠教父之稱，早期的歌詞結合了社會鬥爭和政治抗議，而愛情和宗教也是歌曲中的重要主題。曾獲 12 座葛萊美獎，2016 年更以自己的歌詞榮獲諾貝爾文學獎。

Elton John 艾爾頓強

為英國創作歌手、作曲家、鋼琴家，自 1967 年以來，艾爾頓強爵士與作詞人伯尼陶平成為創作夥伴，迄今二人已經合作完成三十餘張專輯，贏得了六座葛萊美獎盃、四座全英音樂獎獎盃、兩座奧斯卡獎盃、一座金球獎獎盃和一座東尼獎獎盃。

Eric Clapton 艾力克萊普頓

為英國音樂家、歌手及詞曲作家，有「吉他之神」的稱呼。是史上唯一一位 3 度入選「搖滾名人堂」的吉他手和詞曲創作者，他曾經獲得過 18 座葛萊美獎，為 20 世紀最成功的音樂家之一。

folk 民謠

是代表地區、地方或國家的傳統音樂，透過家庭和其他小型社會群體傳承，美國民謠包括藍調音樂、早期鄉村音樂和抗議歌曲。

soft rock 抒情搖滾

是搖滾音樂的一種形式，比 hard rock 更為柔和，旋律優美，也更具商業性。像是木匠兄妹樂團 (The Carpenters) 的 "Close to You"，就屬於抒情搖滾。

Jamie Foxx 傑米福克斯

以喜劇演員身分出道，職業生涯中不但在以自己同名的情境喜劇《The Jamie Foxx Show》演出，也在電影中演出，並推出專輯。在 2004 年傳記電影《雷》中飾演盲人歌手 Ray Charles，並因此獲得奧斯卡最佳男主角獎和英國電影學院獎最佳男主角獎，算是影視歌三棲的藝人。

PHRASES

live under a rock 過原始人的生活

此片語字面上的涵義為「住在岩石底下」，我們用這個片語形容某人「和世界脫節」，不知道世界上發生了什麼事，也不知道最新的趨勢。

A Who's Harry Styles? I've never heard of him.
哈利史泰爾斯是誰？我從沒聽過他。

B Have you been **living under a rock** for the past few years?
你過去幾年都住在山上嗎？

make ends meet 讓收支平衡

此片語照字面上解釋是「使兩端相接」，大家可以想成記帳時「收入」與「支出」兩欄的數字至少要「入能敷出」，才不會還沒月底就月光光、心慌慌，所以 make ends meet 可解釋為「收支平衡、勉強餬口」等。

A How's the pay at your company?
你公司的薪資待遇如何？

B Pretty bad. I'm barely making enough to **make ends meet**.
很差。我幾乎賺不夠錢來維持生計。

(get one's) big break （獲得）大好機會

big break 指的是對於渴望在特定行業或專業工作的人來說，在該行業中獲得了「難得的機會」，像是重要的突破。

◎ The actress **got her big break** when she won a role on the popular TV show.
女演員在贏得一個熱門電視節目的角色後，終於迎來了她的事業突破。

◎ The band's **big break** was being invited to play at a music festival.
這個樂團的重大突破是受邀參加音樂節表演。

across the pond 大西洋彼岸，指美國或英國

這裡的 pond 指的是大西洋，指的是位於大西洋兩側的美國或英國，指代的國家會根據說話者的位置來判斷。若說話者在美國，則他的 across the pond（大西洋彼岸）指代的為英國，反之亦然。

◎ The Beatles were even more popular **across the pond** than they were in the U.K.
披頭四在美國比在英國本土更受歡迎。

◎ We're flying **across the pond** this summer to visit my parents in London.
今年夏天，我們要飛到倫敦拜訪我的父母。

(be) in the public eye （在媒體上）頻頻出現，廣為人知

片語字面上的意思為「公眾視線」，引申為「大眾的關注焦點」，像是電影明星、知名運動選手，甚至是著名罪犯皆是 in the public eye。

◎ The position requires someone who is comfortable **being in the public eye**.
這個職位需要一個能夠在公眾面前感到自在的人。

◎ Movies stars must get used to living their lives **in the public eye**.
電影明星必須習慣在公眾眼光下過生活。

the third time is the charm 第三次也許會成功

用來表示某事已經失敗了兩次，但第三次也許會成功。這個片語用來激勵某人在已經失敗兩次的情況下進行第三次嘗試。

A I can't believe that Steve is getting married again.
我無法相信史蒂夫又要結婚了。

B Well, you know what they say—**the third time is the charm**.
嗯，你知道他們說的——這次說不定他能修成正果。

QUOTES

關於他的招牌紅髮

"I do like my hair. It took a while to come around to the fact that it was quite a unique value point."

我很喜歡我的頭髮。花了一點時間我才想通，頭髮是我非常獨特的價值點。

關於唱歌

"It was my love for the guitar that first got me into music and singing."

我一開始是因為熱愛吉他才對音樂和唱歌產生興趣。

談到自己的人格特質

"I'm quite arty. I didn't know whether to become an artist or musician but I realized I could paint with music. All my songs have colors."

我還蠻喜歡藝術的。我不知道該成為畫家還是音樂家，但我發現我能用音樂彩繪。我的歌裡都有色彩。

歌曲的所有權

"But once you've made a song and you put it out there, you don't own it anymore. The public own it. It's their song. It might be their song that they wake up to, or their song they have a shower to, or their song that they drive home to or their song they cry to, scream to, have babies to, have weddings to--like, it isn't your song anymore."

歌一旦寫出來、發表出去就不是你的了，是大眾財，是大家的歌。可能是他們的起床歌、洗澡歌，開車回家時聽的歌，讓人哭泣、尖叫的歌，生產歌、婚禮歌——就不再是你的歌了。

談論自己的個性

"I've never really been a confident person, except from a musical standpoint. I had to push myself early on, but it got easier with each gig."

如果不從音樂的角度來看，我從來不是個自信的人。我得早早就鞭策自己，但隨著每次演出總是熟能生巧。

關於歌曲風格

"I think the moment you start trying to please a fan base is when you start going downhill. I'm going to always, always write about what I want, even if it doesn't necessarily cater to most of them."

你開始取悅粉絲的那一刻就是你開始走下坡的時候了。我會一輩子寫我想要的東西，就算迎合不了多數粉絲也無所謂。

談論自己的歌壇定位

"I find the whole concept of women screaming at me so odd. It's very flattering, but I don't think I will ever consider myself to be a sex symbol."

我覺得女性對我尖叫實在太奇怪了。我是很開心，但我還真不把自己當成性感偶像。

Billie Eilish
怪奇比莉
腳踏實地的 Z 世代偶像

© Ben Houdijk / Shutterstock.com

身為 Z 世代偶像，比莉以她敢說敢言的風格成為年輕人的表率。才剛以電影《芭比》原聲帶中的歌曲〈What Was I Made For?〉，奪下葛萊美獎的「年度歌曲獎」，比莉又發聲抨擊許多歌手推出多個版本的黑膠唱片，以吸引粉絲購買的舉動，相當不環保。比莉算是非常有膽識！也希望此舉能真正吸引關注並獲得改善。

The Down-to-Earth Gen Z Idol

From an *aspiring dancer to one of the biggest pop stars of her [1]generation, Billie Eilish has been through many stages on the road to fame. Before accidentally injuring her hip at 13, Eilish was a talented [2]ballet and *tap dancer. Although the injury took a toll on Eilish's mental health, she found another passion—singing. Little did she know that the change of focus would lead to **fame and fortune**.

從一個滿懷雄心壯志的舞者，到當代名氣最響亮的流行歌手，艾利許歷經許多階段才功成名就。艾利許原本是個才華洋溢的芭蕾和踢踏舞者，直到十三歲不小心髖部受傷，不能繼續跳舞。受傷影響到她的心理健康，卻讓她找到另一個愛好——唱歌。她哪裡知道，這次的轉換有天會讓她名利雙收。

Eilish, who is *homeschooled, released her first song, "Ocean Eyes," on SoundCloud when she was just 14. Her brother [LG]FINNEAS produced the song, and has continued to work as her *songwriting partner and producer. With its [3]mellow vocals and mature lyrics, "Ocean Eyes" immediately caught the attention of music fans and critics alike. Released as the lead single of Eilish's debut EP, the song eventually received over six billion *streams. It marked the beginning of Eilish's journey as a pop artist.

艾利許兒時在家自學，十四歲在 SoundCloud 音樂平台上面發表自己的第一首歌曲〈海洋雙眸〉，由她哥哥菲尼亞斯歐康諾製作，並持續和她一起創作歌曲、擔任她的製作人。〈海洋雙眸〉憑藉著柔美的嗓音和成熟的歌詞，立即吸引了樂迷和樂評。〈海洋雙眸〉成為她首張迷你專輯的首發單曲，累積超過六十億的播放次數，成為艾利許邁向流行歌手之路的起點。

VOCABULARY

1. **generation** [ˌdʒɛnəˋreʃən] (n.)
   代，世代
2. **ballet** [bæˋle] (n.)
   芭蕾舞，芭蕾舞團
3. **mellow** [ˋmɛlo] (a.) 柔和的

ADVANCED WORDS

* **aspiring** [əsˋpaɪrɪŋ] (a.) 有抱負的
* **tap dancer** [tæp ˋdænsə] (n.) 踢踏舞者
* **homeschool** [ˋhomˌskul] (v.)
  自行在家教育小孩
* **songwriting** [ˋsɔŋˌraɪtɪŋ] (n.) 歌曲創作
* **stream** [strim] (n./v.)（電腦）串流

Following this early attention, Eilish released her first album, *When We All Fall Asleep, Where Do We Go?*, to huge commercial success and __critical acclaim__. Each of the album's singles was certified ^LG)^**platinum**, and three songs achieved ^LG)^**diamond** status. One of these was "Bad Guy," in which Eilish, rather than the song's male character, takes the role of the tough *****troublemaker**.

初步取得成功之後，艾利許發行首張專輯《當我們睡了怪事發生了》，不僅銷售亮眼更獲得普遍好評。專輯每首單曲都獲得白金唱片認證，其中三首取得鑽石唱片的地位，〈壞傢伙〉是其中的一首。在這首歌中，使壞的不是男主角，而是由艾利許來當那個無法無天的麻煩人物。

Songs like this show a ^1)^**confidence** that is rare in one so young. Eilish has also shown she __is her own person__ by supporting the ^LG)^**body positivity** movement. She prefers *****baggy** clothes and refuses to dress like a typical female pop star, which appeals to fans who feel *****self-conscious** about their bodies.

這類歌曲展現的自信，在這麼年輕的歌手身上實在很難見到。確實，從她支持身體自愛運動也可以看出她的獨立自主。她喜歡穿寬鬆的衣服，拒絕一般女歌手的那種裝扮，這一點非常吸引那些對自己身體缺乏自信心的歌迷。

VOCABULARY

1. **confidence** [ˋkɑnfɪdəns] (n.)
   自信，信心
2. **physical** [ˋfɪzɪkəl] (a.)
   身體的，肉體的
3. **costume** [ˋkɑstum] (n.)
   道具服，變裝服

Along with 2)**physical** appearance, Eilish has spoken about mental health issues by revealing that she has LG)**Tourette's Syndrome**. Rather than expressing shame, she openly discusses the condition. Eilish has also talked about suffering from stress and panic attacks during tours, but she's still able to **put on a brave face** for her fans during performances. This attitude gives fans a reason to appreciate Eilish for more than her music.

除了外貌，艾利許也談到心理健康問題，透露自己患有妥瑞症。她公開談論這種疾病，一點也不覺得羞恥。她也談到自己在巡演期間經常恐慌發作，飽受壓力之苦，但是為了粉絲她還是假裝沒事進行表演。粉絲們之所以欣賞她，不僅僅是因為她的音樂，還包括了這種直率的態度。

Examples of Eilish's *****headstrong** personality don't end there. Having received criticism for a relationship with fellow musician LG)**Jesse Rutherford**, who is 11 years older than her, Eilish didn't let these opinions affect her. In response to people who criticized the age gap, Eilish wore a baby 3)**costume** for *****Halloween**, while Rutherford dressed up as an old man.

還有其他例子可以看出艾利許的個性很倔。她和大她十一歲的樂界同行傑西魯瑟福交往招來批評，非但不以為意，反而在萬聖節時穿上嬰兒裝，路瑟福德扮成老爺爺，回嗆那些批評兩人年齡差距的人。

ADVANCED WORDS

* ***troublemaker** [ˈtrʌbəlˌmekɚ] (n.)
  搗亂者，鬧事者
* ***baggy** [ˈbægi] (a.)
  寬鬆而下垂的，袋狀的
* ***self-conscious** [ˈsɛlf ˈkɑnʃəs] (a.)
  害羞扭捏的，不自在的

* ***headstrong** [ˈhɛdˌstrɔŋ] (a.)
  任性的，固執的
* ***Halloween** [ˌhaloˈin] (n.)
  萬聖節前夕

This wasn't the first time the media focused on Eilish's love life. Internet gossip surrounded her previous relationship with actor Matthew Vorce, also 11 years her ¹⁾**senior**. After they broke up, Eilish denied rumors that he had <u>cheated on her</u>. She also complained about a magazine ""[*]**outing**" her for being attracted to women. These experiences led her to highlight the dangers of believing everything on the Internet.

媒體聚焦艾利許的感情生活已經不是第一次。她與同樣大她十一歲的前任男友、演員馬修沃斯交往時，網路就已充斥流言蜚語。兩人分手後，艾利許否認外界所謠傳的男友偷吃。她也抱怨雜誌報導她受女性吸引，害她就這麼「被出櫃」。這些經驗讓她強調盡信網路傳言有害無利。

While Eilish was comfortable dating older men, she also drew attention to the possible ²⁾**abuse** of power that such a situation can create. Her 2021 song "Your Power" describes an older man who uses his position to control a young girl.

儘管艾利許和熟男交往很自在，她仍提醒大家注意這種關係可能產生的權力濫用。2021 年推出的歌曲〈你的權力〉就描述年長男性利用權勢控制年輕女孩的故事。

It's not just human beings that Eilish has helped through her music and influence. As a ³⁾**passionate** ⁴⁾**activist** for animal rights, she encouraged fashion brand Oscar de la Renta to ⁵⁾**ban** fur from their collection at the ^{LG)}**Met Gala** in 2021. Eilish herself is [*]**vegan**, as she maintains that animal ⁶⁾**agriculture** is

---

VOCABULARY

1. **senior** [ˋsinjɚ] (n.) 較年長者，前輩
2. **abuse** [əˋbjus] (n.) 濫用，腐敗的行為
3. **passionate** [ˋpæʃənɪt] (a.) 有熱忱的，熱情的
4. **activist** [ˋæktəvɪst] (n.) 運動人士，活躍人士
5. **ban** [bæn] (v.) 禁止，取締
6. **agriculture** [ˋægrɪˏkʌltʃɚ] (n.) 農業
7. **version** [ˋvɝʒən] (n.) 版本
8. **consume** [kənˋsum] (v.) 吃，喝，消耗
9. **vegetarian** [ˏvɛdʒəˋtɛrɪən] (a./n.) 素食的；素食者

"*horrendous" for animals and the environment. She also partnered with Nike to create a vegan [7]version of the shoe company's original Air Force 1 design.

透過音樂和影響力，艾利許幫助的不只人類。她是熱心的動物平權擁護者，曾促請時尚品牌 Oscar de la Renta 在 2021 年的紐約大都會博物館慈善晚宴服裝中禁用皮草。艾利許本人吃純素，堅持「畜牧業」對動物、對環境都很「可怕」。她也和鞋商耐吉合作，以原始的 Air Force 1 籃球鞋為原型，打造環保的純素版 Air Force 1。

Feeling that people still aren't doing enough, Eilish continues to encourage them to [8]consume less meat. She also supports organizations like the Healthy Students and Earth Act, which promotes the introduction of healthier, [9]vegetarian meals at schools. With the influence that she has over today's youth, her activism could be good news for our planet at a time when climate change is an *imminent threat.

可是她覺得還是沒有看到改變，所以繼續鼓勵大家少吃肉類。她也支持《健康的未來學生與地球法案》等組織，把更健康的素食餐點引進校園。在氣候變遷的威脅迫在眉睫的時代，以她對現在年輕人的影響力，她的行動主義對地球來說可說是個好消息。

ADVANCED WORDS

* **out** [aʊt] (n.)
  揭露（某人）為（同性戀者等）

* **vegan** [ˈvigən] (a./n.)
  吃全素食的，全素食主義者

* **horrendous** [hɔˋrɛndəs] (a.)
  極糟的，可怕的

* **imminent** [ˈɪmənənt] (a.)
  鄰近的，即將發生的

Because of her *down-to-earth personality, Billie Eilish's influence [1]extends beyond her music. Her [2]accessibility has allowed her to create a particularly strong connection to *Gen Z. Eilish has not allowed her fame to make her [3]arrogant or <u>lose touch with</u> everyday issues that normal people, especially teens, face.

由於個性務實，怪奇比莉的影響力超出了音樂領域。平易近人讓她與 Z 世代建立起特別深厚的關係。她沒有因為名氣大而變得傲慢，或與一般人（尤其是青少年）的日常議題脫節。

It's easy to forget that Eilish is still only in her early 20s. This makes her more aware of and sympathetic to the problems that young people in the social media generation face. She's dealt with many of these issues herself and kept her [4]dignity [5]intact. This makes her a role model for many *Zoomers.

我們很容易忘了艾利許也才二十出頭，更明白也更同情活在這個社群媒體世代年輕人面臨的問題。她自己處理過很多這樣的問題，懂得維護自己的尊嚴，是許多 Z 世代人的好榜樣。

VOCABULARY

1. **extend** [ɪkˋstɛnd] (v.) 延伸，伸展
2. **accessibility** [æk͵sɛsəˋbɪləti] (n.) 容易親近
3. **arrogant** [ˋærəgənt] (a.) 傲慢的，自大的
4. **dignity** [ˋdɪgnəti] (n.) 尊嚴
5. **intact** [ɪnˋtækt] (a.) 未受損傷的，原封不動的

ADVANCED WORDS

* **down-to-earth** [͵dauntəˋɝθ] (a.) 務實的，腳踏實地的
* **Generation Z** [͵dʒɛnəˋreʃən zi] (n.) Z 世代，指 1997 年至 2012 年出生的人，又可稱為 **Zoomer**

LANGUAGE GUIDE (LG)

Finneas O'Connell 菲尼亞斯奧康奈爾

艾利許同母異父的哥哥，為作曲人與歌手，幾乎包辦艾利許所有的歌曲創作。菲尼亞斯有時會和艾利許同台表演，他的首張 EP 《Blood Harmony》於 2019 年 10 月發行。

platinum certification 白金認證

全球音樂產業通常根據唱片在零售端銷售或發貨的單位總數，頒發不同級別的唱片銷售認證。通常唱片認證僅頒發給國際發行的作品，並針對專輯銷售的國家或地區單獨頒發。自 2016 年 2 月起，美國唱片協會 (RIAA) 將點播音訊和視訊串流納入計算，列入唱片銷售認證的機制中，訂立認證門檻如下：

媒體	gold 金唱片	platinum 白金唱片	diamond 鑽石唱片
專輯唱片	50 萬張	100 萬張	1000 萬張
單曲專輯	50 萬張	100 萬張	1000 萬張
音樂影片	5 萬次	10 萬次	100 萬次

body positivity 身體自愛

身體自愛倡導者認為體型不應決定一個人的自我價值，鼓勵每個人接受與擁抱自己的身體特徵。此運動主要由黑人和少數族裔婦女帶頭，鼓吹大尺碼的女性也能夠有自信，愛自己的身體。

Tourette's syndrome 妥瑞症

為神經發展性疾病，常發生於 5～15 歲。主要症狀可分為動作型或聲語型抽動，患者可能會產生簡單動作型抽動，像是眨眼、點頭等，或是較複雜的動作，像是觸碰東西、跺腳等。又或是簡單聲語型抽動，像是清喉嚨、咳嗽等。以上行為皆為不自主行為。

Jesse Rutherford 傑西魯瑟福

1991 年 8 月 21 日出生，為美國歌手和詞曲作者，另類搖滾樂團 Neighborhood 和硬派樂團 Valley Girl 的主唱。與樂隊成員一起創作了公告牌另類歌曲排行榜第一名的熱門單曲《Sweater Weather》，並獲得九白金認證。

Met Gala 大都會藝術博物館慈善晚宴

正式名稱為 Costume Institute Gala，是大都會藝術博物館服裝學院的慈善籌款活動，邀請來自電影、時尚、音樂等領域的名人。自 1995 年以來，皆由《Vogue》總編安娜溫圖主持。每年皆有不同的時尚主題，邀請賓客依主題盛裝出席。

PHRASES

fame and fortune 名利，名聲和財富

fortune 為財富，所以可以用 achieve fame and fortune 描述取得了高度成功或名聲。

◎ Although the singer had been making music for many years, she didn't achieve **fame and fortune** until later in life.
儘管這位歌手多年來一直在創作音樂，但直到晚年才獲得了名聲和財富。

◎ **Fame and fortune** do not always lead to happiness in life.
名聲和財富並不總能帶來生活中的幸福。

critical acclaim 廣獲好評

指電影、書籍、音樂獲得評論家的認可和讚揚，critical 為「評論的」，acclaim 的意思為「公開的讚賞」，獲得評論界的讚譽，也就是 win/receive critical acclaim。

◎ Although the pop album sold well, it did not achieve **critical acclaim**.
雖然這張流行專輯銷量不錯，但並未獲得普遍好評。

◎ The artist was not that well known by the public, but his work received **critical acclaim**.
這位藝術家在公眾中並不那麼出名，但他的作品卻受到了好評。

be one's own person 獨立思考，自己做主

指不受他人限制或無須他人幫助就能養活自己的人。當你認可對方的思考或行為獨立自主，就可說「某人 + be one's own person」。

◎ Greta has never followed the latest trends, as she has always **been her own person**.
格蕾塔從未追隨最新潮流，因為她一直都是獨立自主的人。

◎ The teacher told the student to **be his own person** and not worry about what others thought.
老師告訴學生要好好做自己，不要擔心其他人的想法。

put on a brave face 強裝勇敢，裝作不在乎

形容某人在困難的情況下 put on a brave face，就是他們假裝自己很快樂或滿足，但其實他們內心失望或不快樂。

A I can't believe how happy Erica seems, after failing her exams.
我真不敢相信，艾瑞卡考試不及格後看起來怎麼這麼開心。

B I think she's just **putting on a brave face**.
我想她只是在裝出一副堅強的樣子。

▶ 比莉刻意不和其他女歌手一樣，穿著合身衣物，而是常穿超寬鬆衣服，目的是不希望別人有機會批評她的身材。

QUOTES

談論社會對聰明女性的畏懼

"In the public eye, girls and women with strong perspectives are hated. If you're a girl with an opinion, people just hate you. There are still people who are afraid of successful women, and that's so lame."

在大眾眼裡，女性只要持有強烈主張就會被討厭。只要妳是個有見解的女生，大家就是討厭妳。還是有人害怕成功的女性，有夠爛的。

談論拍照不笑的原因

"I hate smiling. It makes me feel weak and powerless and small. I've always been like that; I don't smile in any pictures."

我痛恨微笑，微笑讓我感到軟弱無力而且渺小。我就是這樣的人，我拍照不笑的。

自己寫歌的靈感來源

"There are always going to be bad things. But you can write it down and make a song out of it."

生活永遠會有鳥事發生，不過你可以把它寫成歌。

談論個性

"I've always done whatever I want and always been exactly who I am."

我一直都做我想做的事，一直都做我自己。

"I'm not going to say I'm cool because I don't really feel that. I just don't care at all, and I guess that's what people think is cool."

我不會說我很酷，因為我不這樣覺得。我只是滿不在乎，大概人們覺得這樣很酷吧。

生活經歷對寫歌的幫助

"I wrote my first song at 12 and remember someone asking, 'What were you going through at 12 that you could write about?' I get what you're saying, but 11, 12, 13 were the hardest years of my life. You learn everything. You learn how horrible things feel."

我十二歲寫出第一首歌，有人就問：「十二歲是有什麼經歷可寫？」我懂你的意思，可是十一到十三歲是我一生最艱難的時期，我什麼都學到了，知道事情有多可怕。

不同音樂對自己的影響

"I grew up on the Beatles; I love Linkin Park and Green Day. I heard hip-hop for the first time at 11 and realized what I was missing."

我是聽披頭四的歌長大的，也喜歡聯合公園和年輕歲月。十一歲第一次聽到嘻哈音樂才知道缺乏了什麼。

告訴年輕人要做自己

"It's all about what makes you feel good. If you want to get surgery, go get surgery. If you want to wear a dress that somebody thinks that you look too big wearing, fuck it—if you feel like you look good, you look good."

自己開心很重要。想整型就去整型。想穿洋裝但別人覺得你穿起來很臃腫，去他的，你覺得自己好看就是好看。

SZA
詩莎
謎樣歌后

© Ben Houdijk / Shutterstock.com

若要說這幾年最紅的歌手，絕對會提到 SZA，在第 66 屆葛萊美拿下了最佳 R&B 歌曲、最佳當代 R&B 專輯、最佳流行合唱組合獎，她說作品中流露自己的脆弱，歌詞內容寫實到讓她自己都覺得尷尬，但這樣的誠實就是她在歌曲中想表述的，一起認識她吧。

Keeping Everyone Guessing

From a young age, Solána Imani Rowe, better known by her stage name SZA, was different. Growing up in a mainly white *neighborhood in New Jersey, she always felt <u>out of place</u>. The daughter of a ***Muslim** father and Christian mother, she attended Jewish summer camp. A talented ***gymnast**, she was sometimes the only black athlete at the events she participated in. While her parents did their best to [1]**ensure** she didn't feel like <u>the odd one out</u>, SZA couldn't help but feel like she didn't belong.

本名為索拉娜伊馬尼羅，更廣為人知的是她的藝名詩莎，她從小就跟別人不一樣。她在紐澤西州的一個白人佔多數的社區長大，總覺得自己格格不入。她的父親是穆斯林，母親是基督徒，卻跑去參加猶太人的夏令營。她是很優秀的體操選手，有時候她參加的體操活動只有她一個是黑人。父母已經竭盡所能讓她不要覺得自己是異類，詩莎還是覺得自己不屬於那裡。

Following her father's faith, SZA had a religious [2]**upbringing** and wore a ***hijab** to school as a young girl. After the [LG]**9/11 terror attacks**, however, [3]**discrimination** against Muslims became more common. When she was bullied by classmates, she decided to start dressing like the other kids at her school.

詩莎在宗教的教養環境中長大，跟隨父親的信仰，小時候都是包著頭巾上學。九一一恐怖攻擊事件發生後，歧視回教徒的情況更加普遍，她被同學霸凌，於是決定和其他的孩童穿著同樣的裝扮。

VOCABULARY

1. **ensure** [ɪnˋʃʊr] (v.) 確保，保證
2. **upbringing** [ˋʌp͵brɪŋɪŋ] (n.)
   養育，扶養
3. **discrimination** [dɪ͵skrɪməˋneʃən] (n.)
   差別對待，歧視

ADVANCED WORDS

* **Muslim** [ˋmʌzləm] (a./n.)
  回教的，伊斯蘭教的；回教徒，穆斯林
* **gymnast** [ˋdʒɪmnəst] (n.) 體操運動員
* **hijab** [hɪˋdʒɑb] (n.)
  頭巾（回教女性出門時包裹頭部用）

While SZA still considers herself a Muslim, some fans note that her sexual lyrics and violent music videos seem to [1)]**contradict** her religious beliefs. Indeed, SZA admits that her career path has not always been easy for her [2)]**conservative** parents to accept.

雖然詩莎仍以穆斯林自居，有些粉絲卻發現她的歌詞帶有情色，音樂錄影帶也充斥暴力，似乎與她的宗教信仰相違背。的確，詩莎承認保守的雙親往往很難接受她的職業生涯。

After dropping out of college, SZA worked as a *bartender at a *strip club to pay for time in a studio, where she started recording songs she'd written. This worried her parents, but they've <u>grown to</u> love her music. A viral video from 2018 shows SZA's father Abdul becoming [3)]**emotional** as he sings along to SZA's song "Broken Clocks."

大學輟學之後，詩莎在一間脫衣舞俱樂部當酒保，賺來的錢拿去付錄音室的租金，開始錄製自己寫的歌。父母曾為此感到憂心，不過現在已經愛上她的音樂了。2018 年，詩莎的父親阿布杜在一支影片中跟唱她的歌曲〈壞掉的鐘〉，情緒激動的模樣讓影片一夕爆紅。

Wearing a cap with the name of SZA's first album *Ctrl* on it, Abdul tells his daughter that he loves her music—especially "Broken Clocks." The song is an [4)]**appropriate** choice as it describes SZA's experience working at the strip club while trying to <u>make it</u> as a [LG)]**recording artist**. SZA responded by thanking her dad for his support.

VOCABULARY

1. **contradict** [ˌkɑntrəˋdɪkt] (v.) 矛盾
2. **conservative** [kənˋsɝvətɪv] (a.) 保守的，傳統的
3. **emotional** [ɪˋmoʃənəl] (a.) 情緒化的，多情的
4. **appropriate** [əˋpropriət] (a.) 適當的，恰當的
5. **accompany** [əˋkʌmpəni] (v.) 陪同，伴隨
6. **inherit** [ɪnˋhɛrɪt] (v.) 經遺傳所得
7. **sensitivity** [ˌsɛnsəˋtɪvəti] (n.) 容易感受的體質，敏感性
8. **category** [ˋkætəˌgɔri] (n.) 種類，範疇

阿布杜頭上戴著印有詩莎首張專輯名稱《Ctrl》的棒球帽，告訴女兒他有多愛她的音樂，尤其是這首〈壞掉的鐘〉。這首歌選得很好，正好描述詩莎一面在脫衣舞俱樂部工作，一面努力成為唱片藝人的歷程。詩莎則回應感謝父親的支持。

Equally important is the presence of her mother, Audrey, who frequently 5)**accompanies** SZA to events. SZA says she 6)**inherited** her 7)**sensitivity** from Audrey. This quality is reflected in songs like "LG)**Drew Barrymore**," the lead single from *Ctrl*. Named after the Hollywood actress, who appears in the video, the song is about being an *outcast—a role Barrymore often plays.

母親奧黛麗經常陪詩莎跑活動，她的存在對詩莎來說和父親一樣重要。詩莎說她遺傳了奧黛麗的敏感，這項特質反映在她的一些歌曲如《全面控制》專輯的首發單曲〈茱兒芭莉摩〉。這首歌以好萊塢女演員命名，描述一名被拋棄的人，正是茱兒芭莉摩在電影中經常扮演的角色，她同時也出演了這首歌的音樂錄影帶。

Another important family member for SZA was her grandmother, Norma. Both Audrey and Norma attended the 2018 Grammy Awards, appearing with their famous relative on the *red carpet. Although SZA didn't win in any of the five 8)**categories** she was nominated for, it was a proud moment for all three women, especially as Audrey and Norma both had spoken parts on *Ctrl*.

詩莎人生中的另一個重要家人是奶奶諾瑪。奧黛麗和諾瑪都出席了 2018 年的葛萊美頒獎典禮，和這位名人眷屬一起走紅毯。儘管詩莎入圍五項全數槓龜，這一刻對三個女人來說仍無比驕傲，尤其奧黛麗和諾瑪都參與了《全面控制》的口白部分。

ADVANCED WORDS

* **bartender** [ˋbɑr͵tɛndə] (n.) 酒保
* **strip club** [strɪp klʌb] (n.) 脫衣舞俱樂部
* **outcast** [ˋaut͵kæst] (n.) 被社會（或集體）拋棄的人

* **red carpet** [rɛd ˋkɑrpɪt] (n.) （為迎接貴賓而鋪的）紅地毯，隆重歡迎（或接待）

Following Norma's death in 2019, SZA got a *tattoo of her grandmother's name on her arm. The singer also expressed regret at not spending more time with Norma during her last moments. Instead, SZA was performing on the popular American 1)comedy show LG)*Saturday Night Live.*

諾瑪在 2019 年逝世，詩莎便將奶奶的名字刺在手臂上。對於沒能在諾瑪臨終時多陪陪她，詩莎表示很遺憾。當時她正在美國的熱門喜劇節目《週六夜現場》中表演。

As a *tribute to her grandmother, SZA included Norma's voice at the beginning of the track "Open Arms" from her second album, *SOS*. Reviewers noted that this song, which features rapper Travis Scott, has an *uplifting feeling. In 2)contrast, songs like "Kill Bill" express feelings of 3)rage and 4)revenge. Based on the LG)Quentin Tarantino movie of the same name, the song's video shows SZA 5)ripping her lover's heart out of his chest with her bare hands.

為了悼念奶奶，詩莎在第二張專輯《愛情警報》中的〈張開雙臂〉開頭放了諾瑪的聲音。樂評注意到這首與饒舌歌手崔維斯史考特合唱的曲目有種振奮人心之感。相較之下，〈追殺比爾〉等歌曲就充滿了憤怒和報仇。〈追殺比爾〉以昆丁塔倫提諾的同名電影為創作基礎，從音樂錄影帶中可以看到詩莎徒手將情人的心臟從胸腔挖出來。

While SZA has called *SOS* "angry" music, many songs express feelings of *insecurity or low 6)self-esteem. On the track "Nobody Gets Me," SZA sings about only liking herself when she's with her lover. The need to be loved and to

VOCABULARY

1. **comedy** [ˈkɑmədi] (n.) 喜劇
2. **contrast** [ˈkɑntræst] (n.) 對比，對照
3. **rage** [redʒ] (n.) 盛怒，暴怒
4. **revenge** [rɪˈvɛndʒ] (n.) 報仇
5. **rip** [rɪp] (v.) 撕，扯，摘
6. **self-esteem** [ˌsɛlfəsˈtim] (n.) 自尊

7. **meantime** [ˈminˌtaɪm] (adv.) 同時
8. **hostile** [ˈhɑstɪl] (a.)
   敵對的，不友善的

impress people is evident throughout SZA's work. She's frequently spoken about her fears that people will hate her new material.

詩莎把《愛情警報》稱為「憤怒」音樂，不過許多歌曲表達的卻是不安全感或自卑感。她在〈沒人懂我〉這首歌中唱到，唯有和愛人在一起，她才喜歡她自己。在詩莎的作品中明顯可見需要被愛、需要討好別人的心情。她也常提到害怕人們不會喜歡她的新作品。

This anxiety makes it hard for SZA to complete songs. <u>**On the other hand**</u>, some fans blamed SZA's record label, Top Dawg Entertainment, for the delayed release of *SOS*. The album was announced in 2019, but didn't drop until 2022. In the [7]**meantime**, fans grew impatient. SZA seemed to confirm suspicions that TDE was to blame for the *****holdup** by calling her relationship with the label " [8]**hostile**."

這種焦慮讓詩莎很難把歌曲完成。另一方面，有些歌迷也責怪詩莎的唱片公司 Top Dawg 娛樂延遲發行《愛情警報》專輯。早在 2019 年就宣佈要發行專輯，卻遲至 2022 年才推出。在這段期間，歌迷已逐漸失去耐性。詩莎曾表示她與唱片公司處於「敵對」關係，似乎也證實了大眾的懷疑，Top Dawg 娛樂的確是唱片延遲推出的原因。

ADVANCED WORDS

★**tattoo** [tæ`tu] (n.) 刺青

★**tribute** [`trɪbjut] (n.)
　稱頌，表達敬意的言辭、事物

★**uplifting** [ʌp`lɪftɪŋ] (a.)
　使人振奮的，使人開心的

★**insecurity** [ˌɪnsɪ`kjʊrəti] (n.) 不安全感

★**holdup** [`hold͵ʌp] (n.) 耽擱，延誤

Although frustrating, the delay created a unique type of [1]**interaction**. After SZA posted a short music video to her Instagram account in 2020, fans used it for a [LG]**TikTok dance challenge**. SZA herself participated in the challenge and accepted her fans' name for the song—"Shirt."

雖然令人灰心，專輯的延遲卻創造了一種獨特的互動形式。2020 年，詩莎在 Instagram 的帳號中放了一小段音樂錄影帶的內容，被粉絲拿來做 TikTok 舞蹈挑戰。詩莎本人也加入挑戰，還接受了粉絲為歌曲命的名：〈襯衫〉。

Most of all, what appeals to fans is SZA's *individualism. Her vocal [2]**delivery** ranges from [3]**aggressive** rap to beautiful melodies, and it's hard to *pigeonhole her music. While some songs could be described as R&B, others are almost impossible to define. Through her work with a variety of artists across different *genres, SZA has [4]**expanded** her reach to fans of different ages and tastes.

最重要的一點，粉絲們欣賞的是她的個人獨特性。她的聲音從侵略性的饒舌到優美的旋律都可以駕馭，你很難去歸類她的音樂。有些歌曲可以被歸為節奏藍調，有些幾乎難以定義。她和各種不同音樂類型的歌手合作，這也擴大不同年齡和品味粉絲對她的接受度。

She has also shown herself to be a talented songwriter, helping to create hits for other artists, including Rihanna, Beyoncé, and Niki Minaj. This desire to **push her boundaries** as an artist has kept her fans constantly guessing about her next move.

她也幫蕾哈娜、碧昂絲、妮姬米娜等歌手創作熱門歌曲，證明自己是個才華洋溢的創作者。她渴望突破歌手極限，讓粉絲們猜不透她的下一步會是什麼。

VOCABULARY

1. **interaction** [ˌɪntəˈrækʃən] (n.) 互動
2. **delivery** [dɪˈlɪvəri] (n.) 表演風格
3. **aggressive** [əˈɡrɛsɪv] (a.) 有攻擊性的，侵略性的
4. **expand** [ɪkˈspænd] (v.) 擴大，擴展

ADVANCED WORDS

* **individualism** [ˌɪndəˈvɪdʒuəlˌɪzəm] (n.) 獨特氣質，個人主義
* **pigeonhole** [ˈpɪdʒənˌhol] (v.) 歸類
* **genre** [ˈʒɑnrə] (n.) （藝文作品的）類型

LANGUAGE GUIDE (LG)

9/11 terror attacks
九一一恐怖攻擊事件

2001 年 9 月 11 日發生在美國的一系列襲擊事件，19 名蓋達組織 (Al Qaeda) 恐怖分子劫持 4 架民航客機。將兩架飛機分別衝撞紐約世界貿易中心雙塔的一號大樓（北塔）及二號大樓（南塔），包含飛機上全體乘客、組員及建築物中眾多人群，造成了 2,996 人在此次襲擊中死亡或失蹤。經濟上的影響總額至少為 5 兆美元。

recording artist 唱片藝人

是指以自己的名義錄製和發行音樂的個人和團體，內容可包含唱歌或演奏樂器。錄製音樂後，製作人會編輯這些文件，最終將其發佈為 CD、音樂檔案，有時甚至是黑膠唱片。通常藝人也會巡迴演出以推廣新唱片。世界上幾乎所有最著名的音樂家都是唱片藝人。

Drew Barrymore 茱兒芭莉摩

1975 年出生，是一名美國女演員、電影監製、導演，現為脫口秀《The Drew Barrymore Show》主持人。出生於演藝世家，從小出道，之後主要以喜劇甜心的形象出現。曾拍過《E.T. 外星人》、《婚禮歌手》、《霹靂嬌娃》等膾炙人口的電影。

Saturday Night Live 週六夜現場

美國一檔於周六晚間時段播出的喜劇小品類綜藝節目。於 1975 年 10 月首播，節目諷刺惡搞政治和文化，除了有喜劇演員的搞笑橋段，也會出現人氣歌手在節目上宣傳歌曲，讓節目維持高收視率。

Quentin Tarantino 昆汀塔倫提諾

美國男導演、編劇、監製和演員。其作品常以分格鏡頭，非線性敘事法進行。另外，場景中常有大量的髒話，以及誇張的血腥與死亡場面充斥著黑色幽默的對白。其執導的知名電影包括《追殺比爾》、《惡棍特工》、《從前，有個好萊塢》。

TikTok challenge 抖音挑戰

這是 TikTok 創作者挑戰其追隨者執行某些動作的方式，例如：舞步、lip-syncing（對嘴挑戰最喜歡的歌曲）並於 TikTok 分享，發布者常使用特定主題標籤在 TikTok 上發布這些短影片，以吸引更多人注意。

PHRASES

out of place 感到不自在、格格不入

out of place 的意思是「不合適、不屬於某個地方」，用來形容某人感到不自在或覺得格格不入。

A Have you adjusted to living in the big city yet?
你已經適應在大城市生活了嗎？

B Yeah. I felt **out of place** at first, but I'm used to it now.
是的。起初我感到格格不入，但現在我已經習慣了。

the odd one out 與眾不同的人（或物），異類

odd 為「奇怪的，異常的」，有種遊戲「找出不同的」，名稱就叫做 find the odd one out.

◎ Guess which animal in this picture is **the odd one out**.
猜猜看這張圖片中哪一隻動物是不同的。

◎ Ron was always **the odd one out** at school; he didn't have many friends.
羅恩在學校總是格格不入，他沒有很多朋友。

grow to... 逐漸開始……

要表達一段時間內的情感，可以用「grow to + 動詞」，時態通常會用過去式或是現在完成式，以表達過去的情感或是過去至今的的感覺轉變。

◎ I hated tomatoes as a kid, but I've gradually **grown to** love them.
我小時候討厭番茄，但漸漸地我開始喜歡它們了。

◎ Although I'm still not very friendly with my manager, I've **grown to** respect him.
雖然我和我的經理仍然不太友好，但我已經開始尊重他了。

make it 事業成功

主要的意思為「在工作上取得成功」，另外也有「及時抵達某處、能夠參加活動」的意思。

◎ The actor admitted there were times when he didn't think he'd **make it**.
　這位演員承認有時他覺得自己無法成功。

◎ This book gives readers advice on how to **make it** as a fashion designer.
　這本書為讀者提供了如何成功成為時尚設計師的建議。

on the other hand... 另一方面來說，……

hand 是指所站的位置（也就影響到看事情的角度）。on the one hand 表示「從一個角度來看」，on the other hand 就是「從另一個角度來看」了。除非是要同時強調雙方面的看法，才會先說 on the one hand,... 再說 on the other hand,...（均置於句首），不然通常都是一方面的看法說完之後，接著說 on the other hand,... 就好。

A Social media is really great for sharing news and information.
　社交媒體真的很適合分享新聞和信息。
B **On the other hand**, it's sometimes hard to know what's real and what's fake.
　反過來說，有時很難分辨什麼是真的，什麼是假的。

push (the / one's) boundaries 突破界線

當想要表達嘗試超出自己舒適圈的事情，以獲得更多成長時，可以把這些創新的事物當主詞。也能表達某人以挑戰既定規範或可接受行為的方式行事。

◎ The discovery of the new planet has **pushed the boundaries** of science.
　這顆新行星的發現已經拓展了科學的界限。

◎ When traveling abroad, you should **push your boundaries** by trying new foods.
　在國外旅行時，你應該嘗試新食物來拓展自己的界限。

QUOTES

談論嗜好

"I live in my imagination, so sometimes movies help me get lost. I feel like I'm in it."

我活在自己的想像裡，所以有時候電影會幫助我迷失。我覺得自己置身其中。

自我要求

"I'm a Scorpio with a Pisces moon. I am very critical of myself. I'm actually way less critical of others than I am of myself. I'm in my own head a lot. It's hard and really discouraging."

我是太陽天蠍、月亮雙魚，所以自我批判十分嚴苛。事實上，我對別人的批判比對自己少得多。我常常沉浸在自己的想法裡，很難受，也很令人沮喪。

關於未來規劃

"Every day I grapple between 'I'm going to get married' and 'I'm going to spend the rest of my life alone with a poodle.'"

每天我都在「我要結婚」和「我要和貴賓狗共度餘生」之間拉扯。

關於掌控

"Control is not real, and I'm really understanding that every day. It's about the acceptance of relinquishing control that makes it powerful for you."

控制不是真實的，我每天都在理解這個道理。只有接受交出控制權，你才真正擁有力量。

創作音樂的方式

"Music is my form of cleansing and introspection, so I have to grow in order to accomplish it."

音樂是我淨化和內省的方式，我必須有所成長才能做到。

關於出道成名

"It starts with trusting yourself, even if people are telling you you're too young to trust yourself."

一切都要從相信自己開始，即使有人告訴你，你還太年輕不能相信自己。

男人看待我的方式

"I don't feel ashamed to be loud, which is an argument I've had with lots of men, who thought I was too sassy and unladylike."

我不覺得大聲說話很羞恥，我因為這點和很多男人吵架，他們覺得我很粗魯、不夠淑女。

寫歌靈感

"When your parents regulate everything you hear and everything you intake, it forces you to get creative in other ways. It sparked the writing bug and the very overactive imagination. Because I've had a lot of time by myself and a lot of time isolated from regular culture, I created my own."

當父母控制你所聽到的一切、所吸收的一切時，就迫使你用其他方式發揮創意，這激發了我的寫作熱情和活躍的想像力。因為我獨處的時間很多，與正規文化隔絕的時間很多，反而創造了自己的文化。

Adele
愛黛兒
不妥協天后

© Fred Duval / Shutterstock.com

提到愛黛兒，許多人可能會想到的是她動人的嗓音，和先前略微壯碩的身材。的確，她的身材一直是媒體關注的焦點，但她減肥可不是為了變美，或是為了滿足別人的眼光，這位極具個性的女性知道自己要什麼，看看這位美聲歌手發跡的過程。

Doing Things Her Own Way

With her soulful voice, **1)genuine** personality, and ***determined** attitude, Adele has **carved out** a **2)remarkable** singing career for herself. Still, behind the **3)glamour** lies a story of personal struggle that has been the subject of much media attention. Raised by a single mother in rough parts of London, Adele Laurie Blue Adkins found joy in music from a young age, inspired by famous LG)**blues** and jazz singers like LG)**Etta James** and LG)**Ella Fitzgerald**.

憑藉著悽婉的嗓音、真誠的個性和堅決的態度，愛黛兒為自己開創了一番非凡的歌唱事業。然而光鮮亮麗的背後是個人的奮鬥故事，也是媒體最愛關注的主題。愛黛兒勞瑞布魯阿德金斯生長在倫敦治安敗壞的地區，由單親媽媽撫養長大，從小就從音樂中得到快樂，深受伊特珍和艾拉費茲潔拉等知名藍調和爵士歌手的啟發。

Her path to success was anything but smooth. Despite her talent, Adele was ignored by record labels at the beginning of her career. Several of them told her she would need to drop a few kilograms to achieve fame. In an industry that is so ***obsessed** with image, she was considered ***overweight**. Later on, the fashion designer LG)**Karl Lagerfeld** also called her "a little too fat." Yet Adele remained satisfied with her appearance. She refused to change just to fit expectations, and once said she would only go on a diet to improve her sex life!

她的成功之路一點也不順遂。儘管才華洋溢，愛黛兒歌唱生涯剛起步時卻受到唱片公司的無視。好幾家唱片公司告訴她，想要成名得先減個幾公斤。在一個極注重形象的行業，她這樣算是過重了。後來，時裝設計師卡爾拉格斐也說她「有點太胖了」。儘管如此，愛黛兒仍對自己的外表很滿意。她拒絕為了迎合別人的期望而改變，她曾說只會為了提升性生活的品質而節食！

VOCABULARY

1. **genuine** [ˈdʒɛnjuɪn] (a.)
   真誠的，真心的
2. **remarkable** [rɪˈmɑrkəbəl] (a.)
   非凡的，特別的
3. **glamour** [ˈɡlæmə] (n.) 吸引力，魅力

ADVANCED WORDS

* **determined** [dɪˈtɜmɪnd] (a.) 有決心的
* **obsessed** [əbˈsɛst] (a.) 著迷的，入迷的
* **overweight** [ˌovəˈwet] (a.)
   過胖的，超重的

Adele 愛黛兒 93

Despite rejecting [1]**demands** to *****conform** to the entertainment industry's standards, Adele did lose around 45 kgs over a two-year period between 2018 and 2020. However, she said that this dramatic change was the result of an [2]**addiction** to exercise. Revealing that she **worked out** to deal with anxiety, Adele denied rumors that she had changed her eating habits. "If anything, I eat more than I used to because I work out so hard," she told *British Vogue* magazine.

愛黛兒雖然拒絕唱片公司要她符合演藝界標準的要求，卻在 2018 到 2020 年的兩年期間減掉了四十五公斤。不過她說之所以會有這麼大的轉變，是因為迷上了運動。愛黛兒透漏她靠運動減輕焦慮，否認改變飲食習慣的傳聞。「真要說的話，我這麼努力運動，反而吃得比以前更多了。」她這樣告訴英國《Vogue》雜誌。

Rather than [3]**superficial** considerations such as physical *****attractiveness**, music has always been Adele's main focus. Starting out by performing in local pubs and clubs, she would also play guitar and sing for her friends at the park. This allowed her to gain confidence without too much pressure. In fact, it was a friend who helped get Adele noticed by uploading her demos to *****MySpace** in 2006. Her powerful voice and raw talent caught the attention of [4]**executives** at independent British label XL Recordings, landing her a contract at the age of 18.

比起外貌這種膚淺的東西，音樂才是她最關心的事。她先在地方上的酒吧和夜店表演，作為一個起步，也會在公園彈吉他唱歌給朋友聽。這樣比較沒有壓力，可以慢慢建立自信。事實

VOCABULARY

1. **demand** [dɪˋmænd] (n./v.) 要求，需求
2. **addiction** [əˋdɪkʃən] (n.) 癮頭，成癮
3. **superficial** [ˌsupəˋfɪʃəl] (a.)
   膚淺的，表面的
4. **executive** [ɪgˋzɛkjətɪv] (n.)
   高階主管，經理人
5. **widespread** [ˋwaɪdˋsprɛd] (a.)
   普遍的，廣泛的

上，就是因為有個朋友在 2006 年時把她的試聽帶上傳到 MySpace，愛黛兒才獲得關注。她那爆發力十足的嗓音和歌唱天賦吸引了獨立唱片公司 XL 唱片主管的注意，讓她年僅十八歲就拿到唱片合約。

Before signing with XL, Adele had already released her debut single "Hometown Glory" on a smaller label. This song, which she wrote when she was just 16, took her only 10 minutes to complete. As only 500 copies of the single were *issued on LG)7-inch vinyl, the song failed to chart when first released. When re-released as the fourth single of Adele's debut album *19*, in 2008, the song was nominated for a Grammy. The album itself earned two Grammys and 5)widespread acclaim.

愛黛兒尚未與 XL 唱片公司簽約之前，就已經在一家小唱片公司出過個人的第一支單曲〈榮耀故鄉〉。這首歌是她十六歲時寫的，僅僅花了十分鐘就完成。由於只發行了五百張七吋黑膠唱片，初次發行時沒能登上排行榜。2008 年時，這首歌作為她首張專輯《19》的第四支單曲再次發行，入圍了葛萊美獎。這張專輯贏得兩座葛萊美獎，而且廣獲好評。

ADVANCED WORDS

* **conform** [kən`fɔrm] (v.)
  遵從，遵守（習俗、規定等）
* **attractiveness** [ə`træktɪvnɪs] (n.)
  （長相或聲音）漂亮，誘人

* **MySpace** [`maɪ͵spes] (n.)
  聚友網（一個供人們透過部落格、照片和影片分享個人資訊的網站）
* **issue** [`ɪʃju] (v.)
  核發，發行

Like *19*, Adele's second album was named after her age at the time of recording. The first single and opening track of *21* is "Rolling in the Deep," which became the first song ever to reach five million in ¹⁾**digital** sales. And the second single, "Someone Like You," was the first song of the decade to be certified 6x platinum in both the U.K. and the U.S.

如同《19》，愛黛兒的第二張專輯也是以錄製時的年齡命名。《21》的首發單曲及專輯的開場曲〈墜入深淵〉成為史上第一支數位銷售量達五百萬的單曲。接著發行的單曲《如你》則是十年來首支在英美都獲得六白金認證的歌曲。

While everything seemed to be going perfectly for Adele, she began to experience health issues during this period—most ²⁾**notably** ᴸᴳ⁾sciatica, caused by a fall before a concert.

正當一切似乎進行得很順利時，愛黛兒卻出現了健康問題，影響最大的是一次演唱會前跌倒造成的坐骨神經痛。

Though this painful condition threatened her career, Adele refused to let it stop her from performing. Through *perseverance** and physical ³⁾**therapy**, she was able to manage the ⁴⁾**discomfort** and pursue her passion, even if it meant *waddling** on stage.

這種症狀非常痛苦，嚴重影響到她的歌唱事業，但是愛黛兒不願就這樣停止表演。她堅持不懈地透過物理治療減緩不適，持續追求自己的愛好，就算在臺上步履蹣跚也不放棄。

VOCABULARY

1. **digital** [ˈdɪdʒɪtəl] (a.) 數位的
2. **notably** [ˈnotəbli] (adv.) 尤其，特別
3. **therapy** [ˈθɛrəpi] (n.) 療法，治療，**physical therapy** 即「物理治療」
4. **discomfort** [dɪsˈkʌmfət] (n.) 不舒服，不適

5. **overwhelming** [ˌovəˈwɛlmɪŋ] (a.) 難以抵擋、忍受的
6. **alcoholic** [ˌælkəˈhɔlɪk] (n.) 酗酒者，嗜酒者
7. **sober** [ˈsobə] (a.) 沒喝醉的，酒醒的，沒吸毒的

Following the birth of her son Angelo in 2012, Adele faced another significant challenge: ^{LG)}**postpartum depression**. Despite the joy and excitement that comes with the arrival of a child, Adele struggled with ⁵⁾**overwhelming** feelings of sadness, anxiety, and self-doubt. In interviews, she has <u>shed light</u> on the difficulties of being a parent.

2012 年迎來兒子安杰羅，愛黛兒卻面臨另一重大挑戰：產後憂鬱症。新生兒理應帶來興奮和喜悅之情，愛黛兒卻必須與強烈的悲傷、焦慮和自我懷疑搏鬥。她在訪談中不斷訴說為人母的種種困難。

She has also spoken about drinking problems, admitting she was a "*[*]**borderline** ⁶⁾**alcoholic**" in her 20s. In October 2023, she revealed that she had been ⁷⁾**sober** for several months. This frank announcement was made before a *[*]**sellout** crowd in Las Vegas. Such honesty in <u>confronting her demons</u> has made Adele even more popular with her fans. Many of them see her as a role model for those facing similar issues.

她還談到酗酒的問題，承認自己二十幾歲時曾經是個「邊緣型嗜酒者」。2023 年 10 月的時候，她透露自己已經戒酒幾個月了，而且是在拉斯維加斯的全場觀眾面前坦白的。如此誠實地說出自己正在對抗心魔，讓她更加受到歌迷喜愛。許多粉絲認為她是那些面臨同樣問題的人好榜樣。

ADVANCED WORDS

* **perseverance** [ˌpɝsəˋvɪrəns] (n.)
  堅持不懈，不屈不撓
* **waddle** [ˋwɑdəl] (n.)
  蹣跚而行，搖擺地走
* **borderline** [ˋbɔrdɚˌlaɪn] (a.)
  臨界的，邊緣的

* **sellout** [ˋsɛlˌaʊt] (n.)
  票全部售出的演出（或比賽）

From humble beginnings to her status as an international icon, Adele has come a long way. She has dealt with [1]**celebrity** gossip about her appearance and behavior from her teens to the present. This <u>invasion of privacy</u> is something few of us can imagine. The difficulties of [2]**coping** with this are highlighted in her music. The song "Hello," for example, includes the line "hello from the other side," which Adele has said represents "the other side of becoming an adult, making it out alive from your late teens, early twenties." This sums up the <u>strength of character</u> that continues to [3]**motivate** Adele and the soul that fills her music.

從卑微的出身一路走到國際巨星，愛黛兒有今日的成就相當了不起。她從十幾歲就開始應對關於她外貌和行為的明星八卦，直至今日。這種侵犯隱私的行為是我們很少人能夠想像的。她在音樂中也特別強調處理這些問題的困難。例如〈你好〉這首歌就有一句歌詞「從另一個世界捎來問候」，愛黛兒說這代表「蛻變為大人的另一個世界，從十八九歲、二十出頭的世界好好地走了出來」。這句話總結了持續激勵她人生與音樂靈魂的堅強意志力。

VOCABULARY

1. **celebrity** [sə`lɛbrɪti] (n.) 名人，名流
2. **cope** [kop] (v.) 應對，處理
3. **motivate** [ˋmotə͵vet] (v.) 激勵，激發

LANGUAGE GUIDE (LG)

Blues 藍調音樂

起源於 1870~1900 年間美國南方。最初並沒有特定的音樂形式，單純只是黑人勞工在工作閒暇之餘以歌唱抒發心中苦悶，因早期藍調歌曲多半在描述生活的灰暗面，故稱 blues（原意表示憂鬱）。後來有人把它結合靈歌及其他音樂元素，逐漸演變成現在的藍調音樂。

Etta James 伊特珍

1938-2012 年，美國藍調、R&B 歌手，有傳奇藍調女歌手之稱。她在 1993 年時進入搖滾名人堂、在 2001 年進入藍調名人堂、在 1999 年與 2008 年時也進入過葛萊美名人堂。歌聲充滿能量，成名曲為〈Tell Mama〉、〈At Last〉等。

Ella Fitzgerald 艾拉費茲潔拉

1917-1996 年，美國爵士樂歌手，有 The First Lady of Song「歌唱第一夫人」之稱，她具有高亢洪亮的嗓音、寬廣的音域和出色的演唱技巧，曾獲 13 個葛萊美獎，知名歌曲為〈A-Tisket, A-Tasket〉、〈Misty〉。

Karl Lagerfeld 卡爾拉格斐

1933-2019 年，旅居法國巴黎的德國籍時尚創意總監與時裝設計師，有「老佛爺」之稱，其最知名的職位是擔任香奈兒的領銜設計師兼任創意總監。

7-inch vinyl 7 吋黑膠唱片

7 吋黑膠唱片的轉速為 45 轉，因為播放速度為每分鐘 45 圈。這些唱片的尺寸明顯比專輯唱片 (LP) 來得小，而且旋轉速度也更快。更高的轉速使 45 轉唱片擁有優越的音質，但這也意味著每面唱片只能存儲幾分鐘的錄音，通常用該唱片來發行單曲 (single)。

sciatica 坐骨神經痛

為肌筋膜疼痛症的一種，症狀可能包括：下背痛、臀部和腿感到疼痛，坐下時尤其明顯、單側整條腿針刺般的燒灼感、持續的一邊臀部痛、突然感到抽痛而站不起身、覺得腳麻，不太能動。

postpartum depression 產後憂鬱症

又稱 PPD，是指「新生兒父母在寶寶誕生後的六週內，罹患的憂鬱症」。社會期待、心理壓力，以及照顧寶寶的壓力、伴侶關係等，都是引發產後憂鬱症的原因。症狀包括：焦慮緊張、失去活力、情緒起伏大與負面想法等。

PHRASES

carve sth. out (for oneself) 靠努力開創出，努力贏得、謀得（尤指職位）

carve out 原本的意思是「從石頭或木頭雕刻出來」，現在引申為「為職場打造一席之地」。

◎ The lawyer is working hard to **carve out** a reputation in the legal field.
律師正努力在法律界開闢出一片名聲。

◎ It took the painter years to **carve out** a name for himself in the art world.
畫家花了多年的時間才在藝術界鑿出一席之地。

work out 健身，鍛鍊身體

這個片語若沒有受詞，就是「健身，鍛鍊身體」，work sth. out 為「計算出，想出」，語意有所不同。

A I can't believe how thin and fit Paula is now.
我不敢相信 Paula 現在身材如此苗條健康。

B That's because she **works out** every day.
那是因為她每天都運動。

shed light (on) 釐清真相，讓真相大白

shed 有「散發、流洩」的意思。shed light on「光線照射到……上」，表示讓一件事變清晰。也可以說 throw light on。

◎ The newspaper report **shed light on** the crime problem in our city.
這份報紙報導讓我們市裡的犯罪問題變得明朗了。

◎ Experts hope the flight recording will **shed light on** the cause of the plane crash.
專家希望飛航紀錄能釐清墜機的原因。

confront one's demons 面對心魔，克服恐懼

指「承認並試圖理解在自己生活中持續引起問題的事物」，例如恐懼、缺點、心理創傷、成癮等，也可以說 face one's demons。

A Are you finding it helpful to see a therapist?
你覺得看心理治療師有幫助嗎？

B Yes. He's helping me **confront my demons**.
有。他正在幫我面對我的內心困擾。

invasion of privacy 侵犯隱私

表示他人不尊重某人不公開某些個人訊息的權利。然而公眾人物因為已經將自己置於公眾視野之中，所以他們的個人生活並沒有受到保護。

A I don't think the media should take photos of celebrities with their families.
我認為媒體不應該拍攝名人與家人的照片。

B Yes, it really is an **invasion of privacy**.
是的，這確實是一種對隱私的侵犯。

strength of character 骨氣，意志力

表示精神堅強的狀態，以及能夠承受巨大壓力的能力，會反映在想法、感受和行動。

◎ It takes **strength of character** to admit when you're wrong about something.
能承認自己錯了需要很有骨氣。

◎ Many people lack of the **strength of character** to recover after major failures.
許多人缺乏堅強意志，在重大失敗後無法恢復。

QUOTES

談到自己的身型

"I'm a big personality. I walk into a room, big and tall and loud."

我就是很有存在感。我走進一個房間就是很大隻很招搖。

對成名的想法

"I just want to make music, I don't want people to talk about me. All I've ever wanted to do was sing. I don't want to be a celebrity. I don't want to be in people's faces, you know, constantly on covers of magazine that I haven't even known I'm on."

我只想做音樂,並不希望人們談論我這個人。我就只想唱歌而已,我不想當名人,不想出現在人們眼前,老是登上雜誌封面連自己都不知道。

對八卦的看法

"I no longer buy papers or tabloids or magazines or read blogs. I used to. But it was just filling up my day with hatred."

我已經不再買報紙、小報或雜誌,也不看部落格了。以前還會,但那只是讓我的生活充滿仇恨。

自己的個性

"I love a bit of drama. That's a bad thing. I can flip really quickly."

我喜歡有點戲劇性,這不是好事,我很容易就激動起來。

對自己的想法

"I'm really happy to be me, and I'd like to think people like me more because I'm happy with myself and not because I refuse to conform to anything."

我真的很高興成為這樣的我,我想人們喜歡我是因為我很滿意我自己,而不是因為我不肯迎合任何標準。

自己的上台恐懼症

"I get so nervous on stage I can't help but talk. I try. I try telling my brain: stop sending words to the mouth. But I get nervous and turn into my grandma. Behind the eyes it's pure fear. I find it difficult to believe I'm going to be able to deliver."

我在舞臺上很緊張只好一直講話。我很努力，努力告訴自己的大腦：不要再送話語到嘴巴去了。可是我一緊張就變成我奶奶了。其實我內心是很恐懼的，我很難相信自己可以順利完成表演。

關於寫歌的想法

"If I were a writer and not a singer in 10 years, I don't know how I'd feel about writing really personal songs and getting someone else to sing them."

假如十年後我不做歌手只寫歌，我不知道寫這些很私人的故事給別人唱會是什麼感覺。

關於容貌焦慮

"The focus on my appearance has really surprised me. I've always been a size 14 to 16, I don't care about clothes, I'd rather spend my money on cigarettes and booze."

我真的很驚訝大家把焦點放在我的外貌。我一直都穿 14 到 16 的尺碼，我才不重視衣服，我寧可把錢拿去買菸買酒。

Miley Cyrus
麥莉希拉
從童星、年少輕狂到蛻變成長

© Brian Friedman / Shutterstock.com

飾演迪士尼巨星的麥莉和某些以童星出道的孩子一樣，也曾經在追尋真我的路上迷失，不過專輯《無盡的夏日假期》的好成績，已經向大家證明她不但找回自己，而且即將繼續大放異彩，就讓我們靜觀她的下一步。

From Child Star to Wild Child and Beyond

Born on a Tennessee farm, Miley Cyrus was [1)]**destined** for fame from a young age. Her parents named her Destiny Hope because they believed it was her destiny to bring people hope. But they called her Smiley because of her sunny personality, later shortening it to Miley. Considering her family background—her father is [LG)]**country** singer [LG)]**Billy Ray Cyrus**, famous for his [2)]**smash** hit, "Achy Breaky Heart," and her *****godmother** is country legend [LG)]**Dolly Parton**—everybody thought she would pursue a career in country music.

麥莉希拉出生於田納西州的一個農場，小小年紀就注定要大放異彩。父母替她取名為黛斯特妮霍普，相信她命中注定為人們帶來希望。由於個性開朗，他們就叫她笑臉兒（Smiley），後來縮寫成麥莉（Miley）。她的父親是鄉村歌手比利雷希拉，以一首熱門金曲〈疼痛破碎的心〉走紅，而麥莉的教母就是鄉村傳奇歌手桃莉巴頓。擁有這樣的家世背景，所有人都認為麥莉也會走上鄉村音樂之路。

But Miley had other ideas. When her dad took her to see a stage performance of *Mamma Mia!*, the nine-year-old said, "This is what I want to do, daddy. I want to be an actress." So he <u>pulled some strings</u> to get her a small part in *Doc*, the medical drama he was starring in at the time. Miley also played a small part in Tim Burton's [3)]**fantasy** drama *Big Fish*, but it was her next role that would make her a star.

麥莉可不這麼想。父親帶她去看舞臺劇《媽媽咪呀！》的時候，這個九歲小女孩說：「爹地，這是我想做的事，我要當演員。」父親就運用關係，在當時他主演的醫療劇《Doc》裡替她爭取到一個小角色。麥莉也曾在提姆波頓執導的奇幻片《大智若魚》裡軋上一腳，不過直到下一個角色才讓她成為明星。

VOCABULARY

1. **destined** [ˋdɛstɪnd] (a.) 命中注定的
2. **smash** [smæʃ] (n.)
   大獲成功的歌曲、電影等
3. **fantasy** [ˋfæntəsi] (n.) 幻想，夢想

ADVANCED WORDS

* **godmother** [ˋgɑd͵mʌðɚ] (n.)
   教母，乾媽

During Miley's first audition for the Disney teen ¹⁾**series** ^{LG)}*Hannah Montana*, the producers thought she was too small and too young for the lead role. But she eventually <u>won them over</u> with her big personality and big voice, and even got a part for her father playing, you guessed it, her father! In the show, she plays a girl who leads a double life: typical teenager Miley Stewart by day, and—with the help of a ²⁾**blond** ³⁾**wig**—teen pop star Hannah Montana by night.

麥莉初次參加迪士尼青少年影集《孟漢娜》的試鏡時，製作人覺得她個子太小、年紀也太小，不符合主角的設定。但是她大方爽朗的個性和大嗓門最終還是說服了劇組，甚至還讓她爸演出一個角色，你沒猜錯，就是演她爸！她在劇中飾演一個過著雙重生活的女孩：白天是平凡的少女麥莉史都華，夜晚則戴上金色假髮，搖身成為青少年流行歌手孟漢娜。

When *Hannah Montana* debuted in 2006, it was an instant sensation, winning record *****ratings** for Disney and turning 13-year-old Miley into a teen idol. And over the show's four-season run, it turned her into a pop star in real life as well. Disney released a series of Hannah Montana soundtrack albums, several of which topped the charts, and her performances on the Best of Both Worlds Tour were so filled with screaming fans that people began comparing her to Elvis and the Beatles.

《孟漢娜》於 2006 年首播旋即造成轟動，創下迪士尼的收視記錄，也讓十三歲的麥莉成為青少年偶像。影集播出的四季期間，麥莉也在現實生活中成為流行歌手。迪士尼發行了一系列《孟漢娜》原聲帶，有幾張登上排行榜冠軍。她在兩全其美巡迴演唱會中的表演獲得滿場

VOCABULARY

1. **series** [ˋsɪriz] (n.) 系列，連續
2. **blond** [blɑnd] (a.) 金髮的
3. **wig** [wɪg] (n.) 假髮
4. **anthem** [ˋænθəm] (n.)
   頌歌，國歌，聖歌

粉絲熱烈尖叫，有人開始拿她與貓王和披頭四相提並論。

Yet despite all the success that *Hannah Montana* brought Miley, she began having an identity crisis. Was she Miley or Hannah? Wanting to know if she could succeed <u>on her own terms</u>, she started releasing music under her real name. On her first two albums, *Meet Miley Cyrus* and **Breakout*, she scored top ten hits with pop rock singles like "See You Again" and "7 Things." But it was the lead single from Miley's 2009 EP *The Time of Our Lives*, "Party in the U.S.A.," that <u>put her on the map</u>. The **all-American* party ⁴⁾**anthem** peaked at No. 2 and became so popular that a **petition* was started to make it the new U.S. national anthem.

《孟漢娜》為麥莉帶來這些成就，她卻開始產生自我認同危機。她到底是麥莉還是漢娜？她想知道憑藉自己是否還能一樣成功，於是開始以真名發行音樂。她的前兩張專輯《遇見麥莉》和《無所不能》以〈再見你一面〉和〈七件事〉等流行搖滾歌曲闖進排行榜前十，但是真正讓她聲名大噪的是 2009 年迷你專輯《活得精彩》中的首發單曲〈美國派對〉。這首美式派對頌歌登上排行榜第二，火紅到有人請願定為新的美國國歌。

ADVANCED WORDS

* **rating** [ˈretɪŋ] (n.) 評分，評價
* **breakout** [ˈbrek͵aut] (n.) 越獄
* **all-American** [ͻlǝˈmɛrǝkǝn] (a.) 典型美國式的
* **petition** [pǝˈtɪʃǝn] (n.) 請願書

Miley was now succeeding as Miley, but she still felt trapped by her [1)]**wholesome** Disney image. So she decided to [2)]**declare** her independence on her next album, *Can't Be Tamed*. On the lead single of the same name, she sings over a dance-pop beat, "Have to get my way yep / Twenty four hours a day." She also changed her look, cutting her hair short, [3)]**dying** it blond and wearing *revealing clothing.

麥莉以麥莉的身分取得成功，卻仍覺得受困於迪士尼的乖乖女形象。她決定以下一張專輯《無法抵擋》宣示獨立。在同名首發單曲中，她隨著流行舞曲的節奏唱著：「我要隨心所欲，一天二十四小時做我自己」。同時她也改變外貌，把頭髮剪短染成金色，穿起暴露衣服。

Miley's final break with her good-girl image came with 2013's *Bangerz*. Combining pop with R&B, the album announced a newer, naughtier Miley. How naughty? After performing "We Can't Stop"—another party anthem, but this time with sex and drugs—on the [LG)]**VMAs**, she then joined R&B singer Robin Thicke for a duet of his hit " [4)]**Blurred** Lines." Wearing a flesh-colored *bikini, she [LG)]**twerked** against Thicke and rubbed him with a giant [5)]**foam** finger. And in the video for "*Wrecking Ball," Miley swings around naked on an actual wrecking ball. Many of her fans were shocked, but that didn't stop it from becoming her first No. 1 hit.

2013 年的《青春大爆炸》專輯終於讓麥莉澈底揮別好女孩形象。專輯以流行音樂結合節奏藍調曲風，宣告一個更嶄新、更不乖的麥莉。到底有多不乖？在 MTV 音樂錄影帶大獎上，

VOCABULARY

1. **wholesome** [ˋholsəm] (a.)
   健康的，純潔的
2. **declare** [dɪˋklɛr] (v.) 宣告，宣布
3. **dye** [daɪ] (v.) 染色
4. **blurred** [blɝd] (a.) 模糊的
5. **foam** [fom] (n.) 泡綿，泡沫

她先是演唱了〈青春大暴走〉——又是一首派對頌歌，只不過這次描述的是性愛和毒品——接著和節奏藍調歌手羅賓西克合唱他的名曲〈模糊界線〉。麥莉身穿肉色比基尼貼著西克扭臀擺腰，並拿著一隻巨型泡棉手指在他身上磨蹭。在〈愛情破壞球〉的音樂錄影帶中，麥莉全裸在一顆鐵球上擺盪，震驚無數歌迷，卻還是成為她的第一首冠軍金曲。

But before her fans had time to **get over** their shock, Miley had already moved on. Over the next several years, she continued to change musical styles, from the *psychedelic rock of 2015's *Miley Cyrus and Her Dead Petz*, to the country pop of 2017's *Younger Now* and the LG)glam rock of 2020's *Plastic Hearts*. No wonder she's been given the title of "pop *chameleon."

粉絲們還沒來得及從震驚裡恢復，麥莉早已邁步向前。接下來幾年她不斷嘗試不同的音樂形態，從 2015 年《麥莉希拉和她已逝的寵物們》的迷幻搖滾，到 2017 年《青春進行式》的鄉村流行，以至於 2020 年《塑膠心》的華麗搖滾，難怪她會被封上「流行變色龍」的名號。

ADVANCED WORDS

* **revealing** [rɪ`vi.lɪŋ] (a.)
  （衣服）暴露的
* **bikini** [bɪ`kini] (n.)
  比基尼泳衣
* **wrecking ball** [`rɛkɪŋ bɑl] (n.)
  落錘

* **psychedelic** [ˌsaɪkə`dɛlɪk] (a.)
  迷幻的，幻覺的
* **chameleon** [kə`miliən] (n.)
  變色龍，反覆無常的人

Constant change has also been the [1)]**theme** in Miley's relationships. After a teen [2)]**romance** with fellow Disney star Nick Jonas, she dated model Justin Gaston, and then [LG)]**Liam Hemsworth**—yes, Thor's younger brother! The couple took frequent breaks though, during which she dated actors like Arnold Schwarzenegger's son Patrick and models like Stella Maxwell. Miley has been open about being [*]**gender fluid**, and generous in her support of the LGBTQ [3)]**community**, starting the [LG)]**Happy Hippie Foundation** to assist homeless LGBTQ youth. Miley and Liam eventually got married, and then divorced a year later, an experience she sings about in "Flowers," the No. 1 hit from her 2023 album *Endless Summer Vacation*. The song not only topped the charts in 38 countries, but also won Miley her first two Grammys—Best Pop Solo Performance and Record of the Year!

麥莉的感情生活也是一任換過一任。先是和同在迪士尼的男星尼克強納斯談了一場青少年的戀愛，接著和男模賈斯汀佳斯頓交往，然後是連恩漢斯沃——沒錯，就是雷神索爾的弟弟！兩人分分合合，期間她又交往了包括阿諾兒子派屈克等演員，以及史黛拉麥斯威爾等模特兒。麥莉向來毫不隱瞞她的性別流動，也大方支持多元性別族群，成立快樂嬉皮基金會協助無家可歸的多元性別青年。麥莉和連恩最終步入婚姻，卻在一年之後離婚。在 2023 年發行的《無盡的夏日假期》專輯中，麥莉以冠軍單曲〈花〉娓娓道出這場經歷。這首歌不僅雄踞三十八國排行榜，更為麥莉奪下生涯首座和第二座葛萊美獎——最佳流行歌手和年度製作！

VOCABULARY

1. **theme** [θim] (n.) 主題
2. **romance** [ro`mæns / `ro͵mæns] (n.)
   浪漫，戀愛
3. **community** [kə`mjunəti] (n.)
   社群，社會

ADVANCED WORDS

* **gender fluid** [`dʒɛndɚ `fluɪd] (a.)
  性別流動的

LANGUAGE GUIDE (LG)

country music 鄉村音樂

起源於二〇年代的美國南方鄉村地區，融合了傳統民謠及福音音樂。通常會和五弦琴或是木吉他一起演奏。

Billy Ray Cyrus 比利雷希拉

1961 年出生，美國鄉村音樂歌手與演員。為多白金唱片銷量歌手，曾獲得兩項葛萊美獎。

Dolly Parton 桃莉巴頓

1946 年出生，為美國歌手和女演員，有傳奇鄉村歌手之稱，有十張金唱片與白金唱片銷售紀錄，多次葛萊美獎得主，並獲得終身成就獎。

Hannah Montana 《孟漢娜》

2006 年 -2011 年在迪士尼頻道播出。美國青少年情境喜劇，此影集跨越四個季節和兩部電影，為有史以來最受歡迎的迪士尼節目。

VMA MTV 音樂錄影帶大獎

全名為 MTV Video Music Awards，始於 1984 年的美國流行音樂獎項，獎勵在流行樂和音樂錄影帶方面做出突出貢獻的藝人。

Twerking 電臀舞

1980 年代末在紐奧良嘻哈音樂「bounce music」興起的一種舞蹈，舞者採取低蹲姿態，以臀部帶動整個身體上下、前後舞動。

glam rock 華麗搖滾

始於七〇年代早期的英國，歌手穿著華麗的服裝，艷麗的化妝和髮型，特別是高跟舞台鞋和閃光顆粒與亮片。吸取了泡泡糖流行音樂、硬式搖滾的強烈吉他旋律、重拍節奏和五〇年代的搖滾樂等音樂影響，透過六〇年代末的錄音技術創新讓這些元素滲入。

Liam Hemsworth 連恩漢斯沃

由於哥哥克里斯在電影《雷神索爾》擔任主角 Thor，所以有「雷神弟」稱號。1990 年出生自澳洲，兩個哥哥皆為演員，連恩也追隨哥哥一起前往洛杉磯發展演藝生涯，連恩漢斯沃曾主演《飢餓遊戲》等。

Happy Hippie Foundation 快樂嬉皮基金會

由麥莉希拉創立於 2014 年，旨在幫助無家可歸青年、LGBTQ 青年和其他弱勢群體，致力於在緊急情況或悲劇發生後立即提供救援。

PHRASES

pull (some) strings 暗中運作

「動用關係」英文有個很傳神的說法是 pull (some) strings「把繩子拉一下」。此說法來自木偶表演，每個木偶身上都有很多的細線，只要扯動這些繩子，小木偶就會動起來，這背後拉繩子的人，當然也掌控了舞台上的一舉一動。所以若要形容透過某些關係做某件事情，就可以用 pull (some) strings 這句話。

A Can you help me get a job?
你可以幫我找工作嗎？

B I'll see if I can **pull some strings**.
我去運作一下看看。

win sb. over 說服（某人）、把（某人）爭取過來

這個片語可以把「某人」放在 win 和 over 間，也可放在 win over 後面，通常指把原本不支持的人爭取過來。

◎ He's not sure about the idea, but I'll do my best to **win him over**.
他對這個想法不太確定，但我會盡力說服他的。

◎ The candidates are working hard to **win over** undecided voters.
候選人們正在努力贏得那些中間選民的支持。

on one's own terms 用自己的方式

由於 term 有「期間，條件」的意思，所以 on one's own terms 的意思為「以自己喜歡的方式或時間來進行某事」。

◎ Parents need to let their children live life **on their own terms**.
父母需要讓他們的孩子按照自己的方式來過生活。

◎ If I'm going to leave the company, I want to leave **on my own terms**.
如果我要離開公司，我想按照我的條件離開。

put sb./sth. on the map 使某人／某地出名

如果某人或某地被標住在地圖上，表示這個人或地點很重要或知名，所以 put sb./sth. on the map 就是「讓人、地出名」。

◎ The success of the actor's first film really **put him on the map**.
這位演員第一部電影的成功真正使他出名了。

◎ The hot dog eating contest **put the small town on the map**.
吃熱狗大賽使這個小鎮受到關注。

get over sth./sb. 從（疾病或令人不快的事）中恢復過來，忘掉某人

get over 是指「忘記」，over 有「重新開始」的意思，通常是要人忘記傷痛、不好的記憶，所以片語 get over it 就是要人忘記過去，放眼未來，重新來過，不要計較就「算了吧」。

◎ It took Celia years to **get over** the loss of her child.
西莉亞花了幾年的時間才從失去孩子的悲痛中恢復過來。

◎ How long did it take you to **get over** your first boyfriend?
你花了多久時間忘記你的第一個男朋友？

QUOTES

談到自己的年少輕狂

"I always say the minute I stop making mistakes is the minute I stop learning and I've definitely learned a lot."

我總是說當我停止犯錯的那一刻，就是我停止學習的時候，我確實學了很多。

對當歌手的熱愛

"Those minutes that I'm on stage are the best! Being there and looking at the crowd and seeing their faces, hearing them sing the positive words from the songs."

站上舞臺的時刻是最美好的！在舞臺上望著觀眾，看著他們的臉龐，聽他們唱著正面的歌詞。

關於拍照微笑

"I just stick my tongue out because I hate smiling in pictures. It's so awkward. It looks so cheesy."

我吐舌頭是因為討厭拍照微笑。超尷尬的，看起來很做作。

談及自己的個性

"I never faked anything. I never played the Disney game of smiling and being a princess and then suddenly having a hard time, saying, 'That isn't who I really am.'"

我從不偽裝。我從不玩迪士尼的遊戲，微笑著假裝自己是公主，一遇到困難就說「那不是真正的我」。

談論自己的擇偶條件

"I've got high standards when it comes to boys. As my dad says, all girls should!

I'm from the South—Tennessee, to be exact—and down there, we're all about Southern hospitality. I know that if I like a guy, he better be nice, and above all, my dad has to approve of him!"

我對男生的標準很高。我老爸說的,每個女生都該這樣!我來自南方(確切來說是田納西州),南方人很講待客之道。我知道如果我喜歡一個男人,他最好要待人親切,最重要的是,必須得到我爸認同!

對歌唱的愛好

"My dad says I could sing before I could talk, if that's possible. I was always humming and things like that."

我爸說我還不會走路就會唱歌了,如果可能的話。我總是一直哼哼唱唱之類的。

家人的重要性

"The only people that you really have, that I learned, are your family, because they love you no matter what."

我了解到家人是你唯一真正擁有的人,因為他們無論如何都會愛你。

成名的雙面刃

"It's so much easier to know who you are when there aren't a thousand people telling you who they think you are."

要是沒有一千個人在那裡告訴你他們眼裡的你是誰,你會更容易知道自己是誰。

Taylor Swift
泰勒絲
從鄉村甜心到流行天后

© Brian Friedman / Shutterstock.com

從一位富有野心的鄉村歌手到富比士億萬富翁，泰勒絲走了很遠的路才到今天的地位。她告訴我們，毫不費力的人生只是神話。不要為了努力而感到羞恥。如此有寫歌天分的泰勒絲既是如此，我們又何嘗能夠不努力呢？

Taylor Swift is the biggest pop star in the world, but did you know she started as a country singer? Although her parents worked in ¹⁾**finance**, they <u>had something else in mind</u> for their daughter, naming her Taylor after folk singer James Taylor. Growing up on a Pennsylvania Christmas tree farm, Taylor's earliest memories are of listening to her grandmother—a ²⁾**professional** ³⁾**opera** singer—sing in church. She loved singing songs from Disney musicals as a kid, and when she ran out of words, she made up her own.

泰勒絲是全世界最知名的流行歌手，但你知道她是以鄉村歌手起家的嗎？泰勒絲的父母從事金融業，對女兒卻另有打算，並以民謠歌手詹姆士泰勒的名字為她命名。泰勒絲在賓州的一個聖誕樹農場長大，兒時記憶都是聽著祖母──一名職業歌劇演唱家──在教堂中演唱。她從小就愛唱迪士尼音樂劇中的歌曲，唱到詞窮就自己編。

Songwriting, it seems, came naturally to Taylor. At age 12, she was lent a guitar and taught her first three ⁴⁾**chords**. "That night, I wrote my first song," she laughs. Inspired by the 90s hits of ᴸᴳ⁾**Shania Twain** and ᴸᴳ⁾**Faith Hill**, Taylor ⁵⁾**shifted** her focus from show tunes to country music. The melodies were nice, but it was the stories that captured her imagination.

泰勒絲似乎是天生就會寫歌。十二歲時，有人借她一把吉他並從零教會她三個和弦。「那天晚上我就寫出人生的第一首歌。」她笑說。她受到九〇年代仙妮亞唐恩和費絲希爾的歌曲啟發，將注意力從音樂劇的表演曲調轉向鄉村音樂。音樂的旋律固然動人，但真正吸引她的是歌裡的故事。

VOCABULARY

1. **finance** [ˈfaɪˌnæns] (n.)
   金融，財務，財政
2. **professional** [prəˈfɛʃənəl] (a.)
   專業的，職業的
3. **opera** [ˈɑp(ə)rə] (n.)
   歌劇

4. **chord** [kɔrd] (n.)
   和弦，和音
5. **shift** [ʃɪft] (v./n.)
   轉移；輪班

To help Taylor break into the music industry, her family moved to a suburb of ^{LG)}Nashville—the Country Music ¹⁾**Capital**. And the move soon paid off. After listening to the 13-year-old play a few songs on the guitar, a Sony executive gave Taylor a ²⁾**publishing** deal. She was the youngest songwriter Sony ever signed, but was so good at it she was able to buy a Lexus *****convertible** in her ³⁾**sophomore** year of high school with the money she earned.

家人為了幫助她打入音樂界，舉家搬到鄉村音樂之都納許維爾的市郊。這次搬遷很快獲得回報。聽完這位十三歲女孩用吉他表演幾首歌曲，索尼音樂的主管就和她簽了一份歌詞出版合約。她是索尼音樂所簽下的最年輕創作者，亮眼的表現讓她在高中第二年就用自己賺的錢買了一輛凌志敞篷車。

But Taylor didn't just want to write songs for other singers—she wanted to be a singer. And it wasn't long before <u>opportunity knocked</u>. While performing at Nashville's Bluebird Café in 2005, she caught the attention of ^{LG)}**Scott Borchetta**, a former Universal Music executive who was starting his own label, Big Machine Records. "I <u>was</u> just <u>blown away</u> by her songs," says Borchetta, who signed Taylor as one of his first artists.

然而泰勒絲不僅僅想幫其他歌手寫歌——她還想自己當歌手。沒多久機會上門了。2005年，她在納許維爾的青鳥咖啡館表演，吸引了環球音樂前主管斯科特波切塔的注意，當時他正準備創辦自己的品牌大機器唱片。「她的歌太讓我驚豔了，」波切塔說。而泰勒絲也被他簽下，成為旗下最早的歌手之一。

VOCABULARY

1. **capital** [ˈkæpɪtəl] (n.) 首都，首府
2. **publishing** [ˈpʌblɪʃɪŋ] (v.)
   出版，發行（為現在分詞）
3. **sophomore** [ˈsɑfmor] (a.)
   二年級的，二年級學生的

For her debut album, *Taylor Swift* (2006), the teenager used her own life experiences to write songs about romance and friendship. On the strength of catchy singles like "Our Song" and "Should've Said No," which both reached No. 1 on the country charts, Taylor was soon opening for country superstars like Brad Paisley and Tim McGraw. And the success of *Taylor Swift*—which remained the top country album for 24 weeks and was certified seven times platinum—turned her into a country star too.

2006 年十幾歲的泰勒絲在首張專輯《泰勒絲》中，基於自己的人生經歷寫出描述愛情和友誼的歌曲。由於歌曲琅琅上口，〈我們的歌〉和〈早該拒絕〉雙雙拿下鄉村歌曲榜冠軍，泰勒絲沒多久便開始替布萊德佩斯里、提姆麥格羅等鄉村音樂超級巨星唱開場。《泰勒絲》盤踞鄉村音樂專輯榜首長達二十四週，獲得七白金認證，而這張專輯的成功也讓她躋身鄉村音樂明星之列。

Although country had been good to Taylor, she began to expand into other genres over her next few albums. *Fearless* (2008) and *Speak Now* (2010) explored the themes of teenage romance and *heartbreak in a country pop style. Singles like "Love Story" and "You Belong With Me" had so much *crossover appeal that they topped country *and* pop charts, making *Fearless* the best-selling album of 2009. And with its carefully crafted songs about the ups and downs of young love, *Speak Now* won her Artist of the Year at the 2011 American Music Awards.

ADVANCED WORDS

* **convertible** [kənˋvɝtəbəl] (n.)
  敞篷轎車
* **heartbreak** [ˋhɑrt͵brek] (n.)
  心碎，傷心
* **crossover** [ˋkrɔs͵ovɚ] (a./n.)
  跨界的（音樂、歌手等）

雖然鄉村音樂讓泰勒絲受益良多，接下來幾張專輯她開始涉足其他音樂類型。2008 年《無懼的愛》和 2010 年《愛的告白》採用鄉村流行風格，探索青少年愛戀與心碎的主題。單曲〈愛的故事〉和〈天生一對〉的跨界元素相當具有吸引力，同時拿下鄉村音樂榜和流行音樂榜的冠軍，將《無懼的愛》推上 2009 年的最暢銷專輯。《愛的告白》專輯精心打造的歌曲，刻畫青春愛情的酸甜苦辣，令她奪得 2011 年全美音樂獎的年度藝人大獎。

It was her next two albums, however, that brought Taylor ¹⁾**mainstream** fame. On *Red* (2012), she added electronic elements to her country pop sound. Despite being about ²⁾**toxic** relationships, "We Are Never Ever Getting Back Together," and "I Knew You Were Trouble"—both about men she dated (ᴸᴳ⁾**Jake Gyllenhaal** and ᴸᴳ⁾**Harry Styles**)—were huge hits with fans and critics alike. And then came *1989* (2014), which Taylor called her "first official pop album." Inspired by '80s ᴸᴳ⁾**synth-pop**, it contained the *****megahits** "Shake It Off," "Blank Space" and "Bad Blood," which all hit No. 1 in the U.S., Canada and Australia.

然而隨後的兩張專輯才讓泰勒絲在主流音樂建立名聲。在 2012 年發行的《紅色》專輯中，她將電子元素加入她的鄉村流行聲音。〈絕對絕對分定了〉和〈我知道你是大麻煩〉寫的都是她的前男友（傑克葛倫霍和哈利史泰爾斯），儘管描述的是不健康的愛情，仍獲得歌迷和樂評的廣大迴響。2014 年推出的專輯《1989》被泰勒絲稱為自己的「第一張正式流行音樂專輯」。專輯靈感來自八〇年代合成器流行樂，收錄的超夯單曲〈通通甩掉〉、〈空白〉、〈壞到底〉在美國、加拿大、澳洲都拿下排行榜冠軍。

But fame can <u>be a double-edged sword</u>. In his 2016 single "Famous," rapper

---

VOCABULARY

1. **mainstream** [ˈmenˌstrim] (n./a.)
   主流（的）
2. **toxic** [ˈtɑksɪk] (a.)
   有毒的，不健康的（關係）
3. **refer (to)** [rɪˈfɜ] (v.) 指的是
4. **deserve** [dɪˈzɜv] (v.) 應受（賞罰）
5. **underline** [ˈʌndɚˌlaɪn] (v.) 在下面畫線
6. **assault** [əˈsɔlt] (n.) 攻擊，襲擊
7. **grope** [grop] (v.) 觸摸，伸出鹹豬手
8. **investment** [ɪnˈvɛstmənt] (n.)
   投資（標的）

Kanye West sings, "I made that *bitch famous," 3)referring to when he grabbed the microphone from Taylor at the 2009 VMAs and said Beyoncé 4)deserved Best Female Video more than her. But Taylor is a fighter, and she fought back with *Reputation* (2017), her R&B-influenced sixth album. On the lead single, "Look What You Made Me Do," which topped the charts worldwide, she sings, "I got a list of names, and yours is in red, 5)underlined." Success, as they say, is the best revenge.

然而名聲如同一把雙面刃。饒舌歌手肯伊威斯特在其 2016 年的單曲〈出名〉中唱了一句歌詞：「我讓那婊子出了名」，指的正是他在 2009 年 MTV 音樂錄影帶大獎典禮上奪走泰勒絲的麥克風，並說碧昂絲更有資格獲得最佳女歌手音樂錄影帶的事件。不過泰勒絲也不甘示弱，在 2017 年以其第六張專輯，受到節奏藍調影響的《舉世盛名》回擊。專輯首發單曲〈看是你逼我的〉雄踞各國排行榜，她在歌詞中唱道：「我有一份黑名單，你的名字鮮紅劃了線」。俗話說得好，成功就是最好的報復。

Speaking of revenge, in 2017 Taylor also won a sexual 6)assault case against LG)David Mueller, a DJ who 7)groped her at a public event. And after Big Machine Records sold the *masters of her first six albums to an 8)investment company in 2020, she recorded them all over again, successfully regaining ownership of her music. It's no surprise that Taylor has become a symbol of female *empowerment and success.

ADVANCED WORDS

* **megahit** [ˈmɛgəˌhɪt] (n.)
  非常受歡迎、暢銷的歌曲、電影等
* **bitch** [bɪtʃ] (n.) 母狗，討厭的女人，（非正式）令人不悅的人
* **master** [ˈmæstɚ] (n.)
  （可以複製更多拷貝的）原版

* **empowerment** [ɪmˈpauɚmənt] (n.)
  賦權，使有權力

說到報復，同樣在 2017 年，泰勒絲打贏了一場性騷擾官司，控告 DJ 大衛穆勒在公開場合對她伸出鹹豬手。另外在 2020 年，大機器唱片公司將其前六張專輯的母帶賣給一家投資企業，隨後她將六張唱片全數重新錄製，成功取回音樂所有權。泰勒絲儼然成為女性賦權和成功的象徵，實不意外。

And Taylor's success has continued to grow. *Lover* (2019) and [1]***Folklore*** (2020) were both the best-selling albums of the year in the U.S., and *Midnights* (2022), led by synth-pop single "[2]**Anti**-Hero," made her the first artist to ***monopolize** the top 10 of the *Billboard* Hot 100. *Midnights* also won Best Pop Vocal Album and Album of the Year at the Grammys, bringing her Grammy total to 14! What's her secret? According to Taylor, it's the songs she writes. "My favorite thing in life is writing about life, specifically the parts of life concerning love," she says. "Because, as far as I'm concerned, love is [3]**absolutely** everything."

泰勒絲的成功持續擴大。《情人》（2019）和《美麗傳說》（2020）雙雙成為美國的年度最暢銷專輯，《午夜》（2022）在合成器流行樂單曲〈反英雄〉的帶領下，讓她成為第一位獨占告示牌百大單曲榜前十名的歌手。《午夜》也奪下葛萊美獎最佳流行演唱專輯和年度專輯，為她生涯累積十四座葛萊美獎！她的成功祕訣究竟是什麼？泰勒絲自己表示要歸功於她寫的歌。「我一生中最愛的事情就是書寫生活，尤其是關於愛的部分。」她說，「因為對我來說，愛就是一切。」

VOCABULARY

1. folklore [ˋfokˏlor] (n.) 民間傳說，民俗
2. anti- [ˋæntaɪ] (a.) 反對的，對抗的
3. absolutely [ˏæbsəˋlutlɪ] (adv.)
　　完全，絕對

ADVANCED WORDS

＊**monopolize** [məˋnɑpəˏlaɪz] (v.)
　包辦，壟斷

LANGUAGE GUIDE (LG)

Shania Twain 仙妮亞唐恩

1965 年出生的加拿大女歌手，有鄉村流行女王之稱，在 90 年代引領鄉村音樂跨越流行音樂市場風潮，成為告示牌統計加總「鄉村專輯榜」冠軍週數最多女歌手，目前仍為美國第七暢銷女藝人。

Faith Hill 費絲希爾

1967 年出生，美國歌手及音樂製作人，同樣是以鄉村歌手出道，後來音樂風格轉變，更偏向主流流行樂。曾獲得 5 座葛萊美獎，銷售量突破全球 3000 萬。

Nashville 納許維爾

位於美國田納西州，為美國東南部人口第四大城。被稱作 Music City，全美國的 400 多家唱片公司都集中在此，Nashville 是僅次於紐約的美國第二大音樂出產地。美國鄉村音樂節和全美鄉村音樂獎皆在當地舉辦。

Scott Borchetta 斯科特波切塔

1962 年出生，美國大機器唱片公司集團的創辦人和高階主管。泰勒絲宣稱波切塔未曾通知或是徵求她的許可，就把自己的音樂版權賣給史考特布萊恩經營的唱片公司──Ithaca Holdings。

Jake Gyllenhaal 傑克葛倫霍

1980 年出生，為美國男演員，曾演出《斷背山》、《明天過後》等，曾與泰勒絲在 2010 年交往，但交往一個多月即分手。

Harry Styles 哈利史泰爾斯

1994 年出生，為英國歌手、詞曲作家與演員，曾參加英國音樂選秀節目《X 音素》後，加入了「一世代」(One Direction) 男團擔任主唱，2016 年，哈利推出個人專輯，曾獲多項葛萊美獎。因卓越的穿衣風格聞名。

synth-pop 合成器流行樂

一種音樂流派，主要使用合成器、鼓機和音序器，有時會用它們來取代所有其他樂器。相關曲風有：電音流行 (electropop)、流行舞曲 (dance-pop) 以及夢幻流行 (dream pop)。

David Mueller 大衛穆勒

為美國電台 DJ，2013 年 6 月在泰勒絲巡演期間，兩人受邀見面，當時他用右手抓住泰勒絲的臀部。泰勒絲團隊告訴穆勒的老闆這起事件，讓他被解雇。2017 年穆勒起訴泰勒絲，要求賠償 230 萬英鎊，最終泰勒絲勝訴。

PHRASES

have sth./sb. in mind (for) 想到某人或某事，考慮選擇（某人）做某事

in mind 為「計畫、意圖」，也就是「對於某特定目的，覺得適合的物件或人選」，片語可單獨使用，也可根據前面的是「某事或某人」，來決定後面要加的是事情還是物件。

◎ Do you **have anything in mind** for Robert's present?
對於羅伯特的禮物你有什麼想法嗎？

◎ The manager **has somebody in mind** for the sales position.
經理心中已有業務職位的適合人選。

opportunity knocks 當機會來臨時

這句話出自諺語中的 Opportunity never knocks twice at any man's door.（機會很少會敲兩次門。）或是 Opportunity knocks but once.（好機會只會出現一次。）這個片語指的是平時要做好準備，這樣當機會來臨時，才能確實掌握。

◎ When **opportunity knocks**, you need to be ready.
當機會降臨時，你需要做好準備。

◎ If **opportunity knocks**, then be sure to open the door.
如果機會來臨，你一定要把門打開迎接。

be blown away (by) 令我大開眼界

blow sb. away 就是「使某人驚嘆不已，令某人大為驚奇」，而 sb. be blown away by sth. 即表示「某人對……極為著迷」或「……使某人印象極為深刻、大受感動」。

A I **was blown away** by the Picasso exhibition.
畢卡索展讓我嘆為觀止。

B I thought it was good, but not *that* good.
我覺得是不錯啦，但沒那麼好。

be a double-edged sword 利弊互現的，雙重作用的

片語原本意思為「雙面刃」，引申為某事有正面與負面影響，不完全是正面的。

A Why do you think living in a big city **is a double-edged sword**?
　你為什麼認為住在大城市是兩面刃呢？

B There are more work opportunities, but the cost of living is higher.
　這裡有更多的工作機會，但生活成本更高。

▶ 泰勒絲在 2022 年全美音樂獎中獲得六項大獎，包括年度藝人、最受歡迎音樂錄影帶、最受歡迎流行女歌手、最受歡迎鄉村女歌手、最喜歡的鄉村專輯，以及最受歡迎流行專輯《Red》。她在全美音樂獎的總得獎數已經累積到 40 座，超越麥可傑克森和天后惠妮休斯頓。

QUOTES

自身個性

"I'm the type of person, I have to study to get an A on the test."

我是那種必須很努力才能拿高分的人。

關於人生態度

"If you are lucky enough to find something that you love, and you have a shot at being good at it, don't stop, don't put it down."

假如你夠幸運找到自己喜愛的事,並有機會把它變成擅長的事,千萬不要放棄,要勇往直前。

回應「把前男友寫成歌」這件事

"If I'm gonna write songs about my exes, they can write songs about me. That's how it works."

如果我要把前男友寫進歌裡,他們也可以寫我,規矩就是這樣。

面對酸民的方式

"I never read one hateful thing said about me by some 12-year-old. So I got to live an actual life. And I've kept that mentality. Just because there's a hurricane going on around you doesn't mean you have to open the window and look at it."

我從未看過十二歲小孩對我說的壞話,讓我能夠過著正常生活,我一直保持這種心態。颶風來襲,不代表你得打開窗戶欣賞它。

不被他人定義

"Anytime someone tells me that I can't do something, I want to do it more."

你愈是說我做不到,我就愈是想做。

和媽媽的關係

"My mom and I have always been really close. She's always been the friend that was always there. There were times when, in middle school and junior high, I didn't have a lot of friends. But my mom was always my friend. Always."

我和媽媽向來很親，她一直都是那個不離不棄的朋友。中學和初中的時候我沒什麼朋友，媽媽一直都是我的朋友。一直都是。

粉絲的地位

"Fans are my favorite thing in the world. I've never been the type of artist who has that line drawn between their friends and their fans. The line's always been really blurred for me. I'll hang out with them after the show. I'll hang out with them before the show. If I see them in the mall, I'll stand there and talk to them for 10 minutes."

世界上我最愛的就是歌迷。我不是那種會去劃分朋友和粉絲的歌手，對我來說那個界線一直很模糊。表演結束我會和他們互動，表演之前我也會和他們互動。假如我在購物廣場遇到歌迷，會站在那裡和他們聊上十分鐘。

如何突破自我

"As soon as I accomplish one goal, I replace it with another one. I try not to get too far ahead of myself. I just say to myself, 'All right, well, I'd like to headline a tour,' and then when I get there, we'll see what my next goal is."

每達成一個目標，我會訂下新的目標。我盡量不把目標訂得太遠。我會告訴自己：「好吧，我來辦場巡演吧。」等到達成了，再看下一個目標是什麼。

Cardi B
卡蒂 B
饒舌新天后

© lev radin / Shutterstock.com

以嗆辣直言聞名的卡蒂 B，在紐約的貧民區長大，為了獨立養活自己，甚至不惜去當脫衣舞孃，又努力當上演員與歌手。靠著自己的力量經濟獨立、勇敢做自己。身為人氣最高的饒舌女歌手，她將持續以自信坦率的態度推出更棒的作品。

Belcalis Marlenis Almánzar, better known by her stage name Cardi B, grew up in ^{LG)}**the Bronx**, New York's toughest *****borough** and the birthplace of hip hop culture. Born in 1992 to a father from the Dominican Republic and a mother from Trinidad, she spoke English and Spanish from an early age, which she credits with giving her "such a thick ¹⁾**accent**." Where did she get her unusual name? "My sister's name is ^{LG)}**Hennessy**," she explains. "So everyone used to call me ^{LG)}**Bacardi**, and I started calling myself Bacardi, which was eventually shortened to Cardi B."

貝爾卡莉絲馬倫妮絲阿爾曼薩爾——大家比較熟悉的是她的藝名卡蒂 B——成長於紐約的布朗克斯，那裡是紐約治安最差的行政區，同時也是嘻哈文化的發源地。卡蒂 B 出生於 1992 年，父親來自多明尼加共和國，母親來自千里達島，她從小就講英語和西班牙語，把自己的「重口音」歸咎於這個原因。她怎麼會取一個這麼特別的名字呢？「我妹妹名叫軒尼詩，」她解釋，「大家就叫我百加得，我也開始稱呼自己百加得，最後就縮寫成卡蒂 B 了。」

Living in a dangerous neighborhood, Cardi joined a gang—the ^{LG)}**Bloods**—at 16, but doesn't ²⁾**recommend** it. "Being in a gang don't make you not one dollar," she says. But she was also a ³⁾**decent** student, and learned how to perform while attending the ⁴⁾**Renaissance** High School for Musical Theater and Technology. Raised on Caribbean music and rap, Cardi was also a big Madonna fan, and performed Lady Gaga songs in talent contests.

VOCABULARY

1. **accent** [ˈæksɛnt] (n.) 口音，腔調
2. **recommend** [ˌrɛkəˈmɛnd] (v.) 推薦，建議
3. **decent** [ˈdisənt] (a.) 像樣的，還不錯的
4. **Renaissance** [ˈrɛnəˌsɑns] (n.) （固定大寫）文藝復興，類似的藝文復興運動

ADVANCED WORDS

* **borough** [ˈbɝo] (n.) （紐約市的）行政區，自治城鎮

由於生活在一個危險的社區，卡蒂 B 十六歲就加入幫派「血幫」，不過她不鼓勵大家加入。「混幫派賺不了錢。」她說。她的學業表現卻還不錯，就讀文藝復興音樂劇與技術高中的時候學過表演。卡蒂是聽加勒比音樂和饒舌歌長大的，也是瑪丹娜的超級粉絲，參加才藝比賽唱的是女神卡卡的歌。

Kicked out of the house for fighting with her sister, Cardi enrolled in community college and got a job as a supermarket [1]**cashier** in Manhattan to make ends meet. But she **dropped out** after two semesters and then got fired from her job for giving discounts to friends. On her last day, the supermarket manager gave her some career advice. "He was like, 'You're so pretty, you got a nice body,'" says Cardi. "He told me to go across the street to New York Dolls, the strip club. That's when I started stripping."

卡蒂因為和妹妹吵架被攆出家門。她報名了社區大學，為了維持生計在曼哈頓的一間超市當收銀員。但是才念了兩個學期就輟學，工作也因為偷給朋友折扣被老闆炒魷魚。最後一天上班時，超市經理給了她一些職業發展的建議。「他說：『你長得那麼漂亮，身材又好。』」卡蒂說，「他叫我去對面的紐約娃娃，一家脫衣舞俱樂部。我就從那時候開始跳脫衣舞。」

On her first shift as a stripper, 19-year-old Cardi made more than she did in a week as a cashier. And although she lied to her mom at first, saying she was babysitting for rich families, the money she made lifted her out of poverty and helped her escape an ***abusive** boyfriend. She soon had a big ***following** at the strip clubs she worked at, and she turned that into an even bigger following

---

VOCABULARY

1. cashier [kæˋʃɪr] (n.) 收銀員

2. exploit [ˋɛk͵splɔɪt] (n.)
功績，英勇事蹟

3. exotic [ɪgˋzɑtɪk] (a.)
異國風味的，奇特的，
exotic dancer 為脫衣舞者

4. wit [wɪt] (n.)（說話的）幽默風趣

5. gangsta [ˋgæŋstə] (n.)
幫派成員，為 **gangster** 的非正式拼法

6. chemistry [ˋkɛmɪstrɪ] (n.)
相處和諧，（男女間）來電

on Instagram, where she posted videos about her colorful [2)]**exploits** as an [3)]**exotic** dancer.

那時她十九歲,當脫衣舞孃才第一次輪班就賺得比當收銀員一週還要多。雖然一開始她對媽媽撒了謊,說她在有錢人家當保母,但她的收入讓她擺脫貧窮,並且逃離暴力男友。很快地,她在上班的脫衣舞俱樂部有了一票追隨者。後來她在 Instagram 上面放一些影片,講述自己跳脫衣舞的精彩故事,吸引了更大票的追隨者。

Everybody loved Cardi's big personality and sharp [4)]**wit**, and her bold, aggressive way of speaking sounded so much like rap that she was invited to join the cast of [LG)]*Love & Hip Hop: New York*, a reality show that follows the lives of aspiring rappers. Using the show as a platform to launch her musical career, Cardi dropped her first song, a remix of [*]**reggae** star Shaggy's "Boom Boom," followed by her first video for "Cheap Ass Weave," a [*]**hilarious** track about haters with bad hair. Next came two mixtapes, [5)]*Gangsta Bitch Music. Vol. 1, Gangsta Bitch Music, Vol. 2*, which featured popular songs like "Foreva" and "Lick"—a collaboration with [LG)]**Offset**, a member of hip hop group Migos. Her [6)]**chemistry** with Offset was so strong that the two started dating.

ADVANCED WORDS

[*] **abusive** [əˈbjusɪv] (a.)
　惡行惡語的,虐待的
[*] **following** [ˈfɑləwɪŋ] (n.)
　追隨者,擁護者
[*] **reggae** [ˈrɛge] (n.) 雷鬼音樂
[*] **hilarious** [hɪˈlɛriəs] (a.) 爆笑的

人人都愛卡蒂的爽朗和機智敏銳，大膽又挑釁的說話方式聽起來就好像在唱饒舌，於是她受邀加入了《愛與嘻哈：紐約》的演出陣容。《愛與嘻哈：紐約》是一齣真人實境節目，記錄一些立志成為饒舌歌手的人生活點滴。卡蒂利用節目當作開啟音樂事業的平臺，推出了第一首歌，是雷鬼音樂天王夏奇的〈引爆激情〉混音版。隨後她推出第一支音樂錄影帶〈低價假髮〉，是一首描述黑特頭髮很醜的搞笑歌曲。接著是兩張混音帶《黑幫婊子音樂，第一輯》和《黑幫婊子音樂，第二輯》，收錄了熱門歌曲〈永遠〉和〈走運〉，後者是和嘻哈團體米戈斯成員 Offset 合唱的。她和 Offset 的火花很強，於是兩人開始交往。

By the time Cardi left *Love & Hop Hop* in early 2017, she was ready for <u>the big leagues</u>. Within months, she'd signed a *multi-million dollar deal with Atlantic Records, and that June, she released her debut single, "Bodak Yellow," a big, bold song about her rise from stripper to rapper that *The New York Times* called "the rap anthem of the summer." Inspired by the flow of Florida rapper ^(LG)Kodak Black on his own debut single "No Flockin," "Bodak Yellow" shot to No. 1 on the Billboard Hot 100, making Cardi the first female rapper to ^1)accomplish this *feat since ^(LG)Lauryn Hill did so in 1998 with "Doo Wop (That Thing)."

2017 年初卡蒂離開了《愛與嘻哈》節目，此時她已經準備好躋身巨星之列。幾個月內她就和大西洋唱片公司簽了一份數百萬美元的合約，同年六月發行首支單曲〈博達克黃〉。這首大膽的金曲描述她從一個脫衣舞孃搖身一變成為饒舌歌手的歷程，被《紐約時報》稱為「今夏的饒舌界頌歌」。〈博達克黃〉用的饒舌技巧來自佛羅里達州饒舌歌手柯達布萊克的首張單曲〈不嗑藥〉，並衝上告示牌百大榜首。卡蒂因此成為自 1998 年勞倫希爾的〈鬥舞（那件事）〉之後，首位達成這項成就的饒舌女歌手。

VOCABULARY

1. **accomplish** [ə`kɑmplɪʃ] (v.)
   完成，實現，達到
2. **document** [`dɑkjəmənt] (v.)
   紀錄，留下證明
3. **infectious** [ɪn`fɛkʃəs] (a.)
   有感染力的

Riding a wave of success from "Bodak Yellow," Cardi dropped her debut album, *Invasion of Privacy*, in April 2018. The album, which [2]**documents** her <u>rags-to-riches</u> story and the problems that come with fame—thus the title—was a huge commercial and critical success. A hip hop record with elements of trap, R&B and Latin music, *Invasion of Privacy* debuted at No. 1 on the *Billboard* 200. In addition to "Bodak Yellow," it included the [3]**infectious** Latin hit "I Like It," which also reached No. 1 on the Hot 100. And at the 61st Grammy Awards, Cardi became the first solo female artist to win Best Rap Album.

〈博達克黃〉一鳴驚人，卡蒂趁勢於 2018 年 4 月推出首張專輯《侵犯隱私》。這張專輯記錄了她白手起家的故事，以及成名後隨之而來的問題（反映在專輯名稱），專輯大賣且廣獲好評。《侵犯隱私》是一張帶有陷阱音樂、節奏藍調和拉丁音樂元素的唱片，一推出就空降告示牌二百大專輯榜冠軍。除了收錄〈博達克黃〉，還收錄了感染力十足的拉丁名曲〈我喜歡〉，同樣是一首告示牌百大冠軍單曲。在第六十一屆葛萊美獎頒獎典禮上，卡蒂成為第一位抱走最佳饒舌專輯的獨唱女歌手。

ADVANCED WORDS

* **multi-** [ˋmʌltɪ] (a.)
   多個，許多
* **feat** [fit] (n.)
   功績，英勇事蹟

Since then, Cardi has put out a *slew of No. 1 hit singles, [1]cementing her status as the new Queen of Rap. First came "Girls Like You," a 2018 collaboration with pop rock band Maroon 5. This was followed in 2020 by "WAP," an [2]explicit song about sex—don't ask what WAP stands for—featuring rapper Megan Thee Stallion, and in 2021 by "Up," a power anthem that was nominated for a Best Rap Performance Grammy. Somehow, Cardi has also found time to start a family, marrying Offset and having two kids, and even try her hand at acting, appearing opposite Jennifer Lopez in the 2019 *heist comedy [LG]Hustlers. What are her plans for the future? "I really feel like I should run for president," Cardi says.

此後卡蒂發表了一連串冠軍單曲，奠定了饒舌新天后的地位。首先是 2018 年和流行搖滾樂團魔力紅合作的〈像你一樣的女孩〉，接著是 2020 年和饒舌歌手梅根尤物合唱〈濕濕小可愛〉，一首非常露骨描述性愛的歌曲——拜託不要問歌名是什麼意思。2021 年推出〈Up〉，又是一首強力頌歌，並獲得葛萊美獎最佳饒舌歌手提名。此間卡蒂還有辦法抽空組成家庭，和 Offset 結婚並育有兩名子女，更嘗試演戲，在 2019 年的犯罪喜劇《舞孃騙很大》中和珍妮佛羅培茲同臺飆戲。未來她又有什麼打算呢？「我真覺得我該競選總統。」卡蒂說。

VOCABULARY

1. **cement** [sə`mɛnt] (v.)
   加強、鞏固（地位、關係等）
2. **explicit** [ɪk`splɪsɪt]
   （描繪性或暴力）赤裸裸的，露骨的

ADVANCED WORDS

* **slew** [slu] (n.)
   許多，一堆
* **heist** [haɪst] (n.)
   搶劫，攔劫

LANGUAGE GUIDE (LG)

The Bronx 布朗克斯

為美國紐約市五個行政區之中最北的一個，是美國人口密度第三高的縣。居民主要以非洲和拉丁美洲後裔居民為主，是紐約有名的貧民區。

Hennessy 軒尼詩 / Bacardi 百加得

Hennessy 為法國白蘭地公司，以製造干邑白蘭地聞名。Bacardi 為世界最大的家族私有的烈酒廠商，以其蘭姆酒聞名。這兩個品牌都有悠久的歷史，在各種雞尾酒和飲料中都很受歡迎。

Bloods 血幫

為 1972 年中期成立於美國加州洛杉磯的街頭幫派，主要成員多為非裔美國人，與瘸幫 (Crips) 對立。代表顏色是紅色，喜歡穿著運動服與彰顯幫派色彩的夾克。最常用的血腥符號包括數字「5」、五角星和五角王冠。幫派手勢為顛倒的 OK。

Love & Hip Hop: New York 《愛與嘻哈：紐約》

是 VH1 上真人秀電視影集的原創作品，該劇於 2011 年 3 月首播，是《愛與嘻哈》節目的第一部。內容聚焦於在男性主導的嘻哈世界中工作的女性的日常生活。卡蒂 B 在第六季和第七季為主要演員。

Offset

生於 1991 年，本名為 Kiari Kendrell Cephus，為美國饒舌歌手。原為嘻哈團體米戈斯（Migos）成員，2019 年 2 月發行首張個人專輯。和卡蒂 B 結婚後育有兩個孩子，但卻屢次出軌，兩人多次分分合合、新聞不斷。

Kodak Black 柯達布萊克

1997 年出生，本名為 Bill Kahan Kapri，為美國饒舌歌手與作曲家，他在 2014 年的歌曲〈不嗑藥〉中首次獲得認可。它的成功使他與大西洋唱片公司簽訂了唱片合約，此單曲也在兩年後首次登上 *Billboard Hot 100*。其他專輯也有不錯的成績。

Lauryn Hill 勞倫希爾

1975 年出生，為美國歌手和音樂製作人，曲風為 R&B、靈魂樂等，她於 1998 年推出的首張專輯《勞倫希爾的錯誤教育》（*The Miseducation of Lauryn Hill*）大受好評。近年來希爾因對音樂產業失望而選擇淡出。

Hustlers 《舞孃騙很大》

2019 年的美國犯罪喜劇電影，改編自 2015 年《紐約雜誌》記者潔西卡普斯勒寫的文章。在全球金融風暴的影響下，一群脫衣舞孃為了生存下去，決定詐騙在華爾街上班的白領階級。該劇由珍妮佛羅培茲、吳恬敏、卡蒂 B 演出。

PHRASES

kick out　逐出，開除

意指「強迫某人離開某個地方或組織」，通常是因為某些負面原因，為非正式用語。

◎ Martin got **kicked out** of school for fighting.
　馬丁因為打架被學校開除了。
◎ The corrupt official was **kicked out** of office.
　那個貪污的官員被罷免了。

drop out　退學，退出

drop 為「停止某種活動、開除、離隊」，因此 drop out 表示「停止參與某事」或是「退學」。

◎ It will be hard to find a job if you **drop out** of high school.
　如果你高中沒唸完，將很難找到工作。
◎ The runner **dropped out** of the race after two laps.
　那位選手在跑了兩圈後退出了比賽。

the big leagues　大聯盟，（某運動、行業或活動的）頂級水準

此片語原本的意思為（美國職棒）大聯盟，也就是美國棒球聯盟的最高級別，後來開始用在非棒球相關的意思，指業界頂級水準，競爭最激烈，但也可能獲得最大的成功。

◎ Kevin always dreamed of playing baseball in the **big leagues**.
　凱文一直夢想在大聯盟打棒球。
◎ You have to graduate from a top law school to work in the **big leagues**.
　你必須從頂尖法學院畢業才能在律師界闖出名堂。

(go from) rags to riches　白手起家，從赤貧到富有

rags 為「破舊的布」，指靠自己的努力，從貧窮到致富。

◎ Andrew Carnegie **went from rags to riches**, becoming the richest man in the world.

安德魯卡內基從窮困潦倒到成為世界首富。

◎ J. K. Rowling's **rags-to-riches** story has inspired many young writers.

J.K. 羅琳的白手起家的故事激勵了許多年輕作家。

try one's hand (at)　著手嘗試

用來形容初次嘗試某事，at 後面接想嘗試的新事物。

A I'm thinking of **trying my hand at** a career in writing.

我考慮嘗試以寫作為業。

B Good luck with that!

祝你好運囉！

QUOTES

啟發人生者

"The women that inspire me to be honest are the women that struggle."

說真的，那些啟發我的都是在困境中努力奮鬥的女性。

成名的代價

"I'm not as open as I used to be. I'm a little bit more filtered, and it kind of sucks, but it's the price you pay to get paid."

我不像以前那麼坦率了，現在會謹慎一點，這樣挺糟糕的，但這就是為了賺錢得付出的代價。

"People are afraid to be themselves because people are afraid to be recorded. Everything is being recorded, and everyone is so sensitive. You say something; a section of people will be offended. It's so annoying; you got to be completely censored."

人們怕做自己是因為怕被記錄下來。什麼都會被記錄，而大家又很敏感。你說了一句話，一部分人就被冒犯。有夠煩的，你得非常謹言慎行。

談論個性

"I'm so free-spirited. Everyone has a me inside them: that loud girl that just wanna go, 'Ayyyy!' No matter if you a doctor, a lawyer, a teacher, it comes out."

我是非常自由奔放的人。每個人心裡都有一個我：那個想盡情大喊「嘿！」的女生。不管你是醫生、律師、老師，都會有這樣的一面。

實境節目的雙面刃

"I was a little hesitant to do *Love & Hip-Hop* because sometimes reality TV can be good for your music career and sometimes bad."

我本來有點猶豫要不要加入《愛與嘻哈》，真人實境節目可能對音樂事業有幫助，也可能反而不利。

談論音樂

"I'm a funny person, but I take my music seriously."

我是個幽默的人，但我嚴肅看待我的音樂。

對金錢的態度

"What counts the most for women is having the confidence to make your own money."

女人最重要的就是要有信心自己賺錢。

談論擺脫貧困

"This is my work ethic: I do not want to raise my future kids where I was raised, and I know the only way to do it is working, working, working, working, working."

這是我的工作態度：我不希望未來孩子在我的童年環境中長大，我知道唯一可以實現的方法就是工作、工作、工作、工作、工作。

對自己嗆辣態度的註解

"When you hear my lyrics, you hear the shots that I throw at people. I throw shots because I always been the underdog. I got rejected so many times, and I say it in my lyrics constantly."

你聽我的歌詞，會聽到我狠嗆別人，那是因為我總是處於劣勢，曾被多次拒絕，我在歌詞裡常常提到。

Post Malone
巨星馬龍
饒舌界的搖滾巨星

© Delmiro Junior / Shutterstock.com

馬龍，一個遊走在唱歌、饒舌和民謠搖滾之間的歌手，他稱自己的音樂「無流派」，外型也誠如自己的音樂般，完美結合了嘻哈與搖滾，讓我們透過音樂，了解馬龍略顯害羞外在下的真實內心。

When Post Malone **burst onto the** music **scene** in 2015, there was little doubt about which genre of music he represented. With his gold teeth, braids, and hip hop style, the 19-year-old looked like a typical rap star. The song "White Iverson," which became the lead single from his debut album, showed Malone's [1)]**fascination** with African-American culture.

2015 年當巨星馬龍初闖樂壇時,他代表的音樂類型是無須懷疑的。金牙、辮子頭和一身嘻哈裝束,十九歲的他活脫脫是典型的饒舌歌星。從他的歌曲〈白人艾佛森〉可以看出他對非裔美國人文化的著迷,而這首歌也成為他第一張專輯的首發單曲。

The song's title refers to Malone's [LG)]**cornrows**, which are similar to the [2)]**hairstyle** of former NBA star [LG)]**Allen Iverson**. The ex-Philadelphia Sixers player is himself often [3)]**associated** with hip hop culture. He even recorded his own rap album in 2020, though it was never released.

這首歌的歌名指的是馬龍的一頭小辮子,和前 NBA 球星艾倫艾佛森的髮型很相似。這名過去效力於費城七六人隊的球員本身也和嘻哈文化頗有淵源,甚至曾在 2020 年錄製自己的饒舌專輯,只不過並沒有公開發行。

In another [4)]**reference** to the *****baller**, Malone appeared in the song's video on a basketball court, **shooting hoops** with a white ball. He's also seen [LG)]**doing donuts** in a white [LG)]**Rolls Royce** Ghost, which the rapper says earned him criticism from the car company for using the [5)]**luxury** vehicle the "wrong" way.

VOCABULARY

1. **fascination** [ˌfæsn̩ˈeʃən] (n.)
   著迷,強烈興趣
2. **hairstyle** [ˈhɛrˌstaɪl] (n.) 髮型
3. **(be) associated (with)** [əˈsoʃiˌetɪd]
   (phr.) 有關聯
4. **reference** [ˈrɛfərəns] (n.)
   提及,暗示

5. **luxury** [ˈlʌkʃəri] (a.)
   奢侈的,豪華的

ADVANCED WORDS

*****baller** [ˈbɑlə] (n.) 球員,球星

馬龍在音樂錄影帶中現身籃球場，拿著一顆白色的籃球投籃，也是在指涉這名球員。影片中他開著勞斯萊斯鬼魅車款玩甩尾繞圈，這位饒舌歌手表示車商批評他把這一款豪華轎車「用錯」方式。

The [1]**disapproval** from Rolls Royce didn't stop Malone from <u>**pushing the envelope**</u>. In the video for the 2021 hit "Motley Crew" – his first solo release in two years – Malone raced his Rolls-Royce Cullinan Black Badge around a *****NASCAR** track. The car was worth around US$670,000. In 2018, Malone's US$320,000 Rolls Royce Wraith was [2]**wrecked** in a [3]**collision** while his assistant was driving. A day later, Malone was spotted driving a Phantom—an even more expensive model from his favorite luxury *****automaker**.

勞斯萊斯的不滿並未阻止馬龍挑戰尺度。他為 2021 年熱門歌曲〈克魯小丑〉——暌違兩年的首支個人單曲——拍攝音樂錄影帶時，又開著他的勞斯萊斯黑標庫里南在 NASCAR 賽道上狂飆，這輛車可是價值六十七萬美金。早前於 2018 年時，馬龍價值超過三十二萬美金的勞斯萊斯魅影由助理駕駛時發生車禍，車子給撞個稀巴爛。不料才過一天，馬龍被人看見開著更昂貴的幻影車款，同樣來自他最愛的豪華汽車製造商。

Appearing in the "Motley Crew" video with Malone are fellow artists Ty Dolla $ign, Big Sean, and Tyga. He's collaborated with all three on various projects. Ty is featured in Malone's 2018 hit "Psycho," which became his second No. 1 on the *Billboard* Hot 100. In the video, Malone drives an [LG]**armored personnel carrier** through the desert, while Ty rides inside the military vehicle.

VOCABULARY

1. **disapproval** [ˌdɪsəˈpruvəl] (n.)
   不滿意，不贊成

2. **wreck** [rɛk] (v.) 破壞，毀壞

3. **collision** [kəˈlɪʒən] (n.) 碰撞，相撞

4. **credibility** [ˌkrɛdəˈbɪləti] (n.)
   可信性，可靠性

5. **partnership** [ˈpɑrtnɚˌʃɪp] (n.)
   合夥關係，合作

和馬龍一同出現在〈克魯小丑〉音樂錄影帶的歌手還有泰朵拉尚、大尚恩和泰加。馬龍和三位歌手有過不同的音樂合作。泰朵拉尚曾為馬龍的 2018 年夯曲〈鈔狂〉跨刀演唱，這支單曲讓他二度登上美國告示牌百大單曲榜冠軍。馬龍在音樂錄影帶中駕著一輛裝甲運兵車馳騁沙漠，軍車裡則坐著泰朵拉尚。

The following year, Tyga joined fellow ^{LG)}Compton, California native Roddy Ricch on the remix of Malone's sixth top 10 hit "Wow." Then, in 2020, Malone made a guest appearance on Big Sean's "Wolves."

隔年，泰加和來自加州康普頓的歌手羅迪里奇一同參與了馬龍的第六支排名前十單曲〈哇〉的混音版。接著在 2020 年，馬龍為大尚恩的歌曲〈狼群〉助陣獻唱。

Working with this *roster of rap stars has given Malone ⁴⁾credibility. These musical ⁵⁾partnerships have explored different styles under the hip hop umbrella, including trap and ^{LG)}cloud rap.

和一票饒舌歌星合作讓馬龍在饒舌界取得威信。這些合作嘗試了各種嘻哈音樂風格，包括陷阱音樂、雲霧饒舌等等。

In his musical influences, style, and attitude, however, Malone is as much a rock star as he is a rapper. Early in his career, Malone gave an interview saying that people who want to be moved by music should listen to Bob Dylan rather than hip hop. This should not be a surprise. In 2013, before he became famous, Malone uploaded a video of himself performing Dylan's 1962 song "Don't Think Twice It's

---

ADVANCED WORDS

* **NASCAR** [ˋnæskɑr] (n.)（美國）全國
  運動汽車競賽協會，全名為 **National
  Association for Stock Car Auto Racing**
* **automaker** [ˋɔtoˏmekəʳ] (n.)
  汽車製造商
* **roster** [ˋrɑstəʳ] (n.) 名單

All Right" on acoustic guitar.

不過就他的音樂靈感來源、風格和態度來看，馬龍既是一個饒舌歌手，也是搖滾明星。馬龍在生涯早期接受採訪時提到，想要從音樂中得到感動，就該去聽巴布狄倫而不是嘻哈音樂。他會這樣說並不意外。早在 2013 年的時候，還未成名的馬龍就上傳了自己彈著木吉他、翻唱巴布狄倫 1962 年歌曲〈別多想了，沒事的〉的影片。

Some fans and even other rappers <u>**called out**</u> Malone for these [1]**remarks**, claiming he's using hip hop to achieve fame and fortune without caring about the genre. Denying this, Malone expressed his love for hip hop. His [2]**comments**, he said, were made during a "beer tasting interview" when he was a little drunk. He insisted that, while he is influenced by different musical genres, his roots lie in hip hop.

此言一出，招來部分歌迷和其他饒舌歌手的抨擊，說他利用嘻哈音樂成名致富，卻根本不在乎嘻哈音樂。馬龍否認外界的指責，表達了他對嘻哈音樂的喜愛。他說那些話是他在一場「啤酒品評採訪」中所說的，當時他已經有點醉了。他堅持自己雖然受到不同音樂類型的影響，嘻哈還是他最深的音樂根源。

[3]**Regardless**, many of Malone's songs make [4]**references** to rock music. His 2018 hit "Rockstar," which features U.K.-born rapper 21 Savage, is one example. The first verse mentions Bon Scott and Jim Morrison, lead singers of rock bands AC/DC and The Doors, *respectively. Both singers were known for their wild behavior on and off stage.

VOCABULARY

1. **remark** [rɪˋmɑrk] (n.) 言辭，評論
2. **comment** [ˋkɑmɛnt] (n.) 意見，評論
3. **regardless** [rɪˋgɑrdlɪs] (adv.) 不管，不顧
4. **reference** [ˋrɛf(ə)rəns] (n.) 提及，暗示
5. **evidence** [ˋɛvədəns] (n.)
   證據，跡象

6. **admiration** [͵ædməˋreʃən] (n.)
   欽佩，佩服
7. **contribute (to)** [kənˋtrɪbjut] (v.)
   促成，加重
8. **logo** [ˋlogo] (n.) 商標，標誌
9. **pioneer** [͵paɪəˋnɪr] (n.) 先驅，倡導者

不管怎樣，他的許多歌曲確實提到搖滾音樂，2018 年和英國出身的饒舌歌手 21 薩維奇合作的歌曲〈搖滾明星〉就是一例。這首歌在第一段歌詞中提到了邦史考特和吉姆莫里森，分別是搖滾樂團 AC/DC 和門戶合唱團的主唱，兩名歌手無論臺上臺下都以狂放不羈著稱。

Further [5]**evidence** of Malone's love of rock music can be found in the *aforementioned single "Motley Crew." The name of the song is a tribute to the'80s heavy metal band Mötley Crüe, whose drummer [LG]Tommy Lee appears in the music video as one of the race drivers. During his band's *heyday, Lee was famous for his *hell-raising—a lifestyle that Malone clearly finds appealing. Malone also showed his [6]**admiration** for Lee by [7]**contributing** to the track "Tommy Lee" by Florida rapper Tyla Yaweh in 2020.

而在前面提到過的單曲〈克魯小丑〉中也可以找到馬龍熱愛搖滾樂的證據。歌名本身就是致敬八〇年代重金屬樂團克魯小丑，該樂團的鼓手湯米李也以另一名賽車手的身分出現在音樂錄影帶中。在克魯小丑的全盛時期，李是出了名的愛滋事闖禍——顯然馬龍覺得這種生活方式有魅力。當佛羅里達州饒舌歌手泰拉亞威在 2020 年推出〈湯米李〉的同名歌曲時，馬龍就曾獻聲合唱，對李的崇拜可見一斑。

In addition to his music, Malone's body is also a *testament to the influence of rock stars. Among his many tattoos are images of Nirvana singer Kurt Cobain, country legend Johnny Cash, and—of course—Bob Dylan. The [8]**logo** of British heavy metal [9]**pioneers** Motörhead appears on Malone's arm.

除了音樂之外，馬龍也用身體證明了搖滾明星對他的影響。他身上為數眾多的刺青當中，就

ADVANCED WORDS

* **respectively** [rɪˋspɛktɪvlɪ] (adv.)
  分別地，個別地
* **aforementioned** [əˋforˏmɛnʃənd] (a.)
  前面提到的，上述的
* **heyday** [ˋheˏde] (n.) 全盛期

* **hell-raising** [ˋhɛlˏrezɪŋ] (n.)
  狂野、喧鬧或不節制的行為
* **testament** [ˋtɛstəmənt] (n.)
  證明，證據

包含了超脫樂團主唱寇特柯本、鄉村音樂名人強尼凱許的肖像，當然，怎麼可能少了巴布狄倫。他的手臂還刺了英國重金屬音樂先驅火車頭樂團的標誌呢。

While Malone's ᴸᴳ⁾**body art** reveals his inspirations, he ¹⁾**concedes** that it also hides his insecurity. Calling himself "ugly," he says the tattoos give him self-confidence when it comes to his appearance.

馬龍的身體藝術展現了他的靈感來源，但他也承認刺青是為了掩飾不安全感。他形容自己長得「很醜」，刺青能讓他對外貌有自信。

As a teenager, Malone lacked this confidence and remembers <u>crying himself to sleep</u> every night. He credits music with helping him escape depression. The birth of his daughter in 2022 also changed his life, as it led him to ***curtail** his drinking and partying.

青少年時期的他缺乏這種自信，記得每晚都是哭著睡著的。他認為是音樂幫助他擺脫憂鬱。自從 2022 年女兒誕生，他的人生也隨之改變，開始減少喝酒和跑趴。

Part rapper, part rocker, Post Malone is a bridge between hip hop and hard rock. While some fans wonder where his heart is, others love how he moves between the two ²⁾**realms**.

一半是饒舌歌手，一半是搖滾歌手，巨星馬龍成為嘻哈和硬式搖滾之間的橋樑。一些歌迷想知道他到底心向何處，其他歌迷愛的正是他能夠游走於兩個世界。

VOCABULARY

1. **concede** [kən`sid] (v.) 承認，讓步
2. **realm** [rɛlm] (n.) 界，領域，範圍

ADVANCED WORDS

* **curtail** [kɚ`tel] (v.) 縮減，削減

LANGUAGE GUIDE (LG)

cornrows 貼頭辮

為傳統的三股辮子 (braids) 風格，起源於非洲，可能指的是美洲和加勒比地區的玉米田。頭髮綁的位置非常接近頭皮，編法比別種辮子更緊。這種髮型保留了黑人自我表達和創造力的聯繫，也可以作為一種政治表達。

Allen Iverson 艾倫艾佛森

1975 年出生，美國職業籃球運動員及饒舌歌手，場上位置為得分後衛和控球後衛。1996 年，成為 NBA 史上最矮的選秀狀元，曾獲兩次全明星賽與 NBA 最有價值球員，2016 年入選籃球名人堂。

do donuts 甩尾繞圈

汽車特技的一種，在加速時讓後輪旋轉，而前輪保持靜止。目標是用輪胎在原地畫出一圈又一圈的胎痕，形狀類似甜甜圈，此舉可能導致輪胎因摩擦而冒煙。現已成為許多獲勝車手的賽後慶祝活動的選擇。

Rolls Royce 勞斯萊斯

為英國豪華汽車製造商，於 1998 年成立，為 BMW 的全資子公司運營，是勞斯萊斯品牌汽車的獨家製造商。

armored personnel carrier 裝甲運兵車

縮寫為 APC，又稱為「裝甲運送車」，作用為在戰場上輸送步兵，除此之外，還能運送物資或補給品，必要時也可用來攻擊敵人。

Compton 加州康普頓

位於美國加州洛杉磯市中心以南的城市，該區拉丁裔占七成，黑人占兩成多，貧困率、犯罪率都很高，也是嘻哈音樂的重鎮。

cloud rap 雲霧饒舌

為饒舌音樂的子流派，具有陷阱音樂的多種聲音特徵，並以其朦朧、夢幻和輕鬆的製作風格而聞名。

Tommy Lee 湯米李

1962 年出生的美國音樂家，在重金屬樂隊 Mötley Crüe 擔任鼓手。他在獨奏時會讓整個鼓組旋轉，個人生活方面，除了喝酒吸毒外，曾結過四次婚，其中最知名的一任妻子為潘蜜拉安德森 (Pamela Anderson)，她是《花花公子》封面常客並在影集《海灘遊俠》演出。

body art 身體藝術

指以人的身體作為媒介的藝術形式，型態包含刺青、身體穿刺、人體彩繪等。一些較為極端的身體藝術還包括自殘以及挑戰肉體極限。

PHRASES

burst onto the scene　突然出現，突然獲得名氣、關注或認可

burst onto 為「突然出現」，scene 的意思是「圈子，界，場地」，此片語也可說 burst upon the scene 或是 burst on the scene。

◎ The young actress **burst onto the scene** after being nominated for an Oscar.
這位年輕女演員因獲得奧斯卡提名而一炮而紅。

◎ The police suddenly **burst onto the scene** and began arresting protestors.
警方突然闖入現場並開始逮捕抗議者。

shoot hoops　打籃球

shoot 是「射門，投球」，hoop 為「籃框」，shoot hoops 為輕鬆地投籃，而非比賽性質。

A What are you doing this weekend?
這個週末你有什麼計劃？

B Just **shooting hoops** with a few friends. Want to join us?
只是和幾個朋友打籃球。要一起嗎？

push the envelope　挑戰極限

這個片語最早是用在航空領域，有本關於美國太空計劃的書《太空先鋒》（The Right Stuff）中，多次出現 "push the outside of the envelope" 這個用法，envelope（包絡線）指的是測試飛機性能的極限，在包絡線內飛行，理論上是安全的，現在 push the envelope（挑戰極限）已經不限在飛航領域，而在任何領域都能使用。

◎ The director has really **pushed the envelope** in his recent films.
導演在他最近的電影中確實挑戰了極限。

◎ The company's new airplane design is an attempt to **push the envelope**.
公司的新飛機設計是為了挑戰極限而做出的嘗試。

call sb. out　斥責，譴責

call sb. out 表示引起他人關注某人的不良行為，藉由公開談論，或直接面對這個人，並具體談論對方做錯了什麼。

◎ These days, celebrities are often **called out** on social media if they do anything wrong.
　現在，名人如果做錯事往往會在社交媒體上受到譴責。

◎ Joel was **called out** by his friends for being rude to the new student.
　喬爾因對新生沒禮貌而被朋友斥責。

cry oneself to sleep　哭到睡著，某人對某事感到不安

此片語其中一個意思就是字面上的意思，形容某人一直哭，直到睡著。另一種是表示某人對某事感到不安，但是是以諷刺的方式。

A Your little brother must be really sad about his dog dying.
　你的小弟一定對他的狗狗去世感到非常傷心。

B Yes, he's been **crying himself to sleep** every night.
　是的，他每晚都哭著入睡。

QUOTES

談論獨處

"In order to find yourself, who you really are, you got to be with yourself; you got to hang out with yourself."

你必須跟自己相處，才能找到真正的自己。你得多跟自己泡在一起。

人生的挫折

"There's always gonna be setbacks; there's always gonna be knockdowns. There's always gonna be people telling you, 'Hey, you suck!'"

總是會有挫折，總是會被擊倒。總是會有人告訴你：「嘿，你爛透了！」

談論自己的癮頭

"You don't know what someone is going through, and you don't know how easy it is just to get caught up in something to the point where you can't stop…"

你並不知道別人正在經歷什麼，你不知道陷入一件事裡無法自拔有多麼容易……

投入音樂的契機

"I started making music... I guess I was 12, and I started playing *Guitar Hero*. And you know, it got to a point where on expert, you can only exceed to a certain point. And so, you know, I was like, 'Let's play real guitar. Let's not waste more time.' So, I got my mom, I told her to buy me a guitar for Christmas, and I started making music then."

我開始做音樂……好像是十二歲吧，我開始玩《吉他英雄》。玩到專家等級之後，到了某一點就很難超越了。然後啊，我就想：「不如來彈真的吉他吧，不要浪費時間了。」所以我就拜託我媽買吉他送我當聖誕禮物，從此就開始做音樂了。

想做的音樂

"I'm trying to bring a little bit of every type of sauce into one type of sound. Something that's really fresh."

我想在一種聲音中每種調味料都各加一點，做出很新鮮的東西。

自己風格的註解

"It's not normal for a white guy to get cornrows; a lot of people judged me. I like the way it looks, so you have to be confident."

白人很少會編貼頭辮，很多人批評我。可是我喜歡這個樣子，就要有自信。

影響的曲風

"In New York, my dad raised me to listen to everything like hip hop, rock and country music. When I moved to Dallas, I started listening to whatever I wanted to listen to."

還在紐約的時候，我爸從小讓我接觸各種不同音樂類型，像是嘻哈、搖滾、鄉村等等。搬到達拉斯之後，我開始聽自己想聽的音樂。

提到童年

"I didn't have no friends or nothing; I was a nerdy kid."

我小時一個朋友也沒有，我是個宅男。

向 A 咖西洋歌手學英文：閱讀人生故事與名言 /EZ TALK
編輯部, Judd Piggott, James Baron 著；丁宥榆譯. -- 初版.
-- 臺北市：日月文化出版股份有限公司, 2024.06
152 面；16.7X23 公分 . -- (EZ talk)
ISBN 978-626-7405-60-4（平裝）
1.CST: 英語 2.CST: 讀本
805.18   113004193

EZ TALK

向A咖西洋歌手學英文：巨星的人生故事與名言

作　　者：EZ TALK編輯部、Judd Piggott、James Baron
譯　　者：丁宥榆
責任編輯：潘亭軒
封面設計：白日設計
封面插畫：PanDaAn
內頁設計：白日設計
內頁排版：簡單瑛設
行銷企劃：張爾芸
錄音後製：采漾錄音製作有限公司
錄 音 員：Jacob Roth、Leah Zimmermann
照片出處：Shutterstock、Wikimedia Commons

發 行 人：洪祺祥
副總經理：洪偉傑
副總編輯：曹仲堯
法律顧問：建大法律事務所
財務顧問：高威會計師事務所

出　　版：日月文化出版股份有限公司
製　　作：EZ 叢書館
地　　址：臺北市信義路三段151號8樓
電　　話：(02)2708-5509
傳　　真：(02)2708-6157
客服信箱：service@heliopolis.com.tw
網　　址：www.heliopolis.com.tw
郵撥帳號：19716071日月文化出版股份有限公司

總 經 銷：聯合發行股份有限公司
電　　話：(02)2917-8022
傳　　真：(02)2915-7212
印　　刷：中原造像股份有限公司
初　　版：2024年6月
定　　價：350元
I S B N：978-626-7405-60-4